Y0-BQA-427

Katzenjammered

a work of fiction

Norma Kassirer

BlazeVOX [books]

Buffalo, New York

Katzenjammered by Norma Kassirer

Copyright © 2010 Norma Kassirer

Published by BlazeVOX [books]

All rights reserved. No part of this book may be reproduced without the publisher's written permission, except for brief quotations in reviews.

All characters in this book are fictional and any resemblance to persons, living or dead, is purely coincidental.

Printed in the United States of America

Book design by Geoffrey Gatza

First Edition
ISBN: 978-1-60964-021-7
Library of Congress Control Number 2010908300

BlazeVOX [books]
303 Bedford Ave
Buffalo, NY 14216

Editor@blazevox.org

publisher of weird little books

BlazeVOX [books]

blazevox.org

2   4   6   8   0   9   7   5   3   1

B   X

Acknowledgments

Many thanks from the author for invaluable help from—

Edric Mesmer
Geoffrey Gatza
Michele Mortimer

Katzenjammered

For my dear friend
Ann — with much
love — Norma

At 2:45, our fire increased in intensity,
and silently we prepared to go over.
Fresnoy, France, May 9, 1917
Pte. Martin Gresham

One pull was carved in a pear shape and there was an apple, cherries, a peach. The two small drawers at the top had grape pulls, very real looking, my father liked to point out; a fine, noble chest of drawers he called it, made by his grandfather on the farm in Canada of cucumber wood from their own forest. That was the place with the trout stream and the wide skies my father dreamed through the Great War. That was before I was born, when he was Private Martin Gresham of the Princess Pats, fighting the war that would end war forever.

His father, said Agnes, was a real horror. She was my mother. An agnostic of the fallen Protestant variety, she distrusted any intimation of the hierarchical, and preferred her first name to a title, even one so universal as Mother. My father, although he also called himself agnostic, was not so fundamental about it. So it was that he was Daddy, she Agnes.

One of the horrible things Grandfather Gresham had done was to sell that farm. And this while his only son was in a military hospital in England—two years with shell shock and a broken back, and all that time yearning for what his father had not bothered to tell him was gone. Never mind that my father wouldn't have lived there anyhow after Aunt Emmy introduced him to Agnes, who was definitely not the sort to live on a farm, didn't know what in the world cucumber wood was, for lord's sake, she used to say. My father didn't either. It was what they called it back then and he'd never thought to ask.

The chest was too big for the room he called his den, which also contained an easy chair, rolltop desk, and of course, his typewriter. My father wanted everything—Agnes said so. And there was no wall space in there, for heavens sake, with the door to the hall, the one to the attic, a window to the front and another to the side that looked into the next door lady's house. She was the one with the fur coat that matched her dachshund, and so stuck up she'd cross the street so she wouldn't have to speak to you. Agnes said the coat was mink, ridiculous she said, to walk a dog in.

It was so crowded in that room, how could a man think, much less write?

The deadly silence was weird
I braced my foot on the scaling
ladder, set my teeth firm, and
waited.
             Pte. M. G.

I find the key in one of the little grape drawers at the top. It fits the peach drawer at the bottom, but I forget about the lady next door, and lo and behold, as Aunt Emmy often says, there she is, in that mink coat. She's staring straight at me. I stare back, my hands full of papers from the drawer. Her lips move, and though I can't hear her through the two layers of glass that separate us, I know what she's saying, that I have no right to be in here snooping in my father's office. I pull the green shade and cancel her.

After that, I put the shade down first, when I come in, so I can read IN PRIVATE, what my own father wrote about the War, in articles that were clipped from Canadian newspapers, and pages torn from Canadian magazines published by the army. PEPANDGO, a shiny-papered magazine published by the insurance company my father works for, is there too.

I close my eyes and leaf through the papers until I feel like stopping. I take out whatever my hand is on and read it. There is always a moment when I pray, well not really PRAY, just hope, very hard, that it won't be the one about my father stumbling over the German soldier with his head blown off.

I know the poem in PEPANDGO by heart.

The Man Who Wins

The man who wins is the average man,
Not built on any particular plan,
Not blessed with any particular luck,
Just steady and earnest and full of pluck,

For the man who wins is the man who works,
Who neither labor nor trouble shirks,
Who uses his hand, his head, his eyes,
The man who wins is the man who tries.

The rhythms are good for masturbating. My friend Gladys told me what that was. She knows everything, though she isn't much older than me. I'm scared of her because she has no limits. She'll do anything. Agnes says she's crazy, and it's no wonder, with what goes on over there.

This is in 1932. I'm nine. My name is Martha, for no good reason. Up until my generation, people in Agnes' family had been named for the people who came before them. Even earlier, they'd been named for virtues, like charity and prudence. Agnes wants nothing to do with any of that. The passing on of names smacks, as she would put it, (she often uses mildly violent imagery, as if she feels pursued by something she knows is going to get her some day) of organized religion. It makes her itch all over, she says.

Far down the line a whistle sounded.
The officer shouted an order, and over
we crawled, into the fumes of cordite
in "no man's land."
         Pte. M. G.

The house is white, the shutters green. There are matching yews on either side of the front stoop. Mr. Rose, the block gardener, who is really Mr. Ross, but has an herbaceous sense of humor, never gets them just right; no one could, a fact that nags at me just beneath the surface of everything else. (I don't notice until adolescence that the shutters are fake and are consequently not wide enough to cover the windows.) Stella, who is the maid, polishes the brass knocker on the front door every morning.

Uncle Flavius had given us the table in the front hall, the one that holds the telephone, which resembles a daffodil in shape and posture. The table is ebony with intricate mother-of-pearl insets, and, according to Agnes, is extremely valuable. Uncle Flavius is an artist. This means that he has good taste, except in wives. In that case, he is simply wise. Aunt Charlotte is rich, an excellent thing in an artist's wife, says Agnes.

Flavius Josephus, I know, is more or less from the bible. There'd been lots of ministers, generations of them, on Agnes's side of the family, but they were all gone by the time she became an agnostic. Essy and Donald and I (I'm the oldest, Donald the youngest) have never set foot in any Sunday school, and never will, not if Agnes has anything to say about it. Some people, she says, need to be herded into churches. She knows how to behave without that sort of prop. We don't have our tonsils out either and will never be inoculated for smallpox, not because of being agnostic exactly; it's simply another intelligent decision, says Agnes. Doctor Billy Martin, at school, always gives the nurse a funny look when he examines me. Well, he says, I see that Martha still has those tonsils. I know by heart why he doesn't mind making me feel bad. He's mad at the whole family because long ago he was engaged to marry my cousin Miranda and she broke it off the day before when all the arrangements had been made for the wedding—you know Miranda.

Jumping across shell holes,
stumbling over dead bodies and
equipment, we ran along.
              Pte. M. G.

Inside the stairs, in the closet in the dark, I hear how they walk, drumbeats that make the wire hangers ring on the metal bar over my head, or soft, like wings, as if the stair wood has turned to air. Up in the den, the peach drawer words stir and hiss, break into syllables, come down one syllable a stair, BAY O NETS FIXED TO RE PEL THE EN E MY. I am part of the stair spine itself, in the mothball, hot-wool-cat-smell, me smelling the smell of myself and liking it. Listening to Agnes talking on the phone. *Well*, she says, my *mother's* idea of *economy* was olive sandwiches. Honestly! she says. Hmmmm, she says. She laughs. Can you *feature* it? she says.

I know that story. I know all the stories. Hers always have a lot of underlinings.

The body lay very naturally
in the field and the stump of
his head was covered with dirt.
Pte. M. G.

Aunt Charlotte had given us the desk in the upstairs hall. It reminds Agnes of Charlotte, expensive, spindly-legged and useless. The green blotter with the brown leather corners is never ink-stained. It is changed when it fades. The desk's job is to hold the lamp with the green glass shade, the blue bowl of tiny white stones mixed with Essy's, Donald's and my lost teeth and the feather pen stuck in among them. The pen has never been used. It is just for decoration.

Our parents' room is across the hall from the feather pen. There are little lamps with orange silk shades in here. The shades do magic things with the light against the dark walls. Everything smells of perfume, even the clock with radium numbers that glow green in the dark, and the two high beds side by side, heaped with comforters and extra pillows. The cat has scooped a cradle out of the bottom of the springs of my father's bed. Venetian blind light and shade stripe the beds and the walls and the floor.

I am in that room. I open the drawers of the small table between the beds. The gun is still there. I knew it. I for my father's bed, KNEW for the table, IT for my mother's. Each syllable broken into light and shadow.

He was wounded, but I
dared not let him live.
          Pte. M. G.

Great Aunt Emmy's daughter Miranda went to finishing school in New Orleans where she was valedictorian of her class and had red hair so long she could sit on it. Why would anyone want to? Agnes wonders.

There were no schools suitable for Miranda in Blue Fields, Nicaragua, where Doctor and I lived in great happiness for so many glorious years until one of those silly revolutions chased us out and everything went straight to hell, excuse me darling, says Aunt Emmy. She calls herself Mrs. Doctor Marshall with servants and department store clerks. Agnes says, She's your father's aunt, not mine.

Sundays, Aunt Emmy and Doctor have dinner at our house. Aunt Emmy always gets drunk as a skunk, she says so herself. Doctor won't drink, it's against the law. Essy and Donald and I are katzenjammered—my father's word for stomach-down on the German oriental reading the Sunday funnies. Player piano doing Two Little Girls in Blue, Lads, the fake Ming vases humming along. Aunt Emmy in a black dress, long pearls, pokes me with a patent leather toe tip. Never mind, darling, she says, never mind. It's what she always says. I'm the one she loves. I know it, everyone knows. I look the way Aunt Emmy used to and wishes she still could. I give her a smile from the floor by way of recompense. Oh, you'll end in Hollywood, she whispers, with thrilling emphasis. She whirls and bumps a vase, it teeters and she catches it and makes a dance of balancing, hugging that Ming thing to her as if it's someone she loves; not me, this time, anyone can see. And certainly not Doctor.

I plunged my bayonet into
his body and closed my eyes.
        Pte. M. G.

I'm shelling peas on the rustic table in the garden. One pea says to the other, Olive sandwiches, that was my mother's idea of economy. A gooseberry says, Was that when she was poor, Pea dear? Yes, olives! Can you feature it? They cost the earth, you know! Did you know she gave me away?

Gave you away, poor dear! Oh, my god, what kind of mother would do that?

She was a fool, no backbone.

Oh my, no backbone! And you were only eight years old?

My father died, and she just fell apart. Some children are fortunate. They're eight and their fathers are around working very hard and their mothers are sensible.

Enter Green Tomato. You went to live with your grandfather, dear?

Oh yes, he was rich, that was my mother's excuse, she said he could give me what a girl ought to have.

What about your brothers?

Like peas in a pod, olives in a jar, they stayed home and were poor. My mother wouldn't accept help from my grandfather except for necessities. Olives, for instance.

I surprise myself with that peas in a pod, olives in a jar. It seems very clever to me. It has emerged somehow from my mother's habit of ironic emphasis.

Olives! the peas all shriek, Olives! Oh my god, those olives! What a fool that woman was!

I heard you say a bad thing, Martha! Essy says from the sandbox. I'm going to tell.

You're lying. What did I say? Prove it.

You said, my god.

Now you said it, now I'm going to tell!

Essy begins to wail.

A sunflower shrieks in a terrible witchy voice that even scares me—That one in the sandbox takes after her grandmother! We call her Olive!

Essy's screaming now. She's having one of her fits. I let Stella take care of it. I'm too shaken by that creepy sunflower.

I was conscious of his warm
Blood, running down my hand.
    Pte. M. G.

Great Grandfather in sepia on the wall over Agnes's bed looks like God.

Oh, how your mother loved him, I say to Donald, in a voice that thrills me from top to bottom; it's the sort I imagine a preacher might use.   Donald looks down at his hands.

Pay attention, Donald, you could grow up to be like him if you stop wetting your pants.

Donald looks unhappy.

You did it again, Donald! If you go on like this, you'll be poor with Agnes and eat olive sandwiches, but I'll rescue you, don't cry, Donald, Martha will take care of you.

Donald's face puckers.   He cries without making any sound.

Stay here, Donald, don't move, I'll tell you what I'll do, as soon as I get out of high school I'll come home and get a job no matter how my grandfather begs me not to; he loves me and I love him, he calls me the little Marchioness, it's in Pinocchio. It's in his own hand-writing.   He gave it to me for Christmas.

That's not your book, that's Agnes's, says Donald.

Shut up, Donald.   Listen, I hate my grandmother, Donald.

You don't hate anyone, Martha! Don't talk that way! Shame on you!

I hate you, Stella! You sneaked in! You didn't even knock!

Go to your room, young lady! And I'm telling your mother about this, you kept poor Donald from going to the potty again. Look at that, he peed all over your mother's rug!

You said pee! I'm telling Agnes! It's ignorant!

And then, suddenly, as I watched,
they came, not in fine charging
line, but in veritable droves.
            Pte. M. G.

The story was that my great grandfather begged Agnes to go to Syracuse University, he even had her all registered, and she might have done it if she'd had a normal life, which, as she often remarks, she never did, of course. No, she marched straight back home after her graduation from high school, to help her mother and her brothers and she got a job on the draft board and that was where she met Aunt Emmy, who introduced her to her nephew when he came back from the war and they fell madly in love. That's Aunt Emmy's version. Agnes says that if her own mother hadn't been such a hapless fool, she wouldn't have been working at the draft board and never would have met my father—she would have gone to Syracuse and had a career and would never have married anyone. She would have been too smart by then.

That grandmother of Agnes's! We all know about her! What a snob! No wonder Agnes hated her! She belonged to the DAR and she was a Suffragette and President of the WCTU and she drank whisky every single day with a WCTU ribbon pinned to her lapel! She pretended it was medicine! Her husband saw right through her. He called her Jake, to tease her about being a Suffragette—why, she was just like that woman in Bleak House who helped all the African children while her own went around with runny noses and earaches. Then my great grandmother wouldn't speak to my great grandfather. She had no sense of humor, that woman. Also, she was jealous of Agnes. Her Christian name, can you feature it?—was America!

They swarmed over the trench
and came at a jog trot towards
our position.
        Pte. M. G.

Quite often I find crumpled paper on the den floor with Buried Alive typed at the top. Usually, there is a line or so of text, but sometimes just the title heading a blank page. I knew that my father had written something called Buried Alive long ago for a military magazine called The Bulletin.

Agnes tells him he should stop thinking about it. She has one of the crumpled sheets in her hand when she says it, so I know that's what she means—Stop thinking about being buried alive. My father doesn't answer. He closes the den door. Agnes stands there in the hall for a while and then she turns around and throws the crumpled paper into the wastepaper basket under the Aunt Charlotte desk. Then she farts.

When Agnes sees me standing there in my nightgown so late, she slaps me. What are you doing? she yells, Get back in bed, you little sneak!   I do get back in bed, but I lie there in the dark thinking how she's just like her horrible grandmother, maybe even worse. Probably, I tell myself, her grandmother never farted, thinking she was alone.

My father doesn't read to Essy or to Donald. Essy is too restless. Donald is too young. My father reads to me. He reads Alice. He reads David Copperfield.

The black and white pictures scare me, but I don't mention it.

Seated in his lap, I smell the sweet pipe tobacco smell of him, feel the scratchy tweed. I compare the tan of his skin with mine. The same sort of skin, a mole on the cheek, as if we are marked for one another, blue eyes, black hair. When he calls me his Old Standby, it is as if he is speaking in code. No one else understands. Not Essy, not Donald. My father cannot get along without me.

There is a shiny brown jug on the sideboard in the dining room. The jug holds whisky. Its stopper is a monk's head and its round body represents his brown robe and rope belt. It is really a music box that plays How Dry I Am whenever it is tipped to pour. Agnes gave it to him for a joke. He never winds it, except when we are alone, and that is another joke. He winks at me when he turns the key. The jug sits next to us on the end table while he reads to me. Agnes is away. When he shifts me in his lap and picks it up and pours the whisky into his glass and it plays its silly little tune, he winks at me again.

*I was crouching on the fire
step, shells of all caliber
bursting around me. I heard
a big one coming.*
        Pte. M. G.

Listen, Donald, listen, be very quiet, if Stella finds out you're in here—listen to this, Father wrote this—I remember seeing a German with his head blown off clean as a whistle. The body lay very naturally on the field and the stump of his head was covered with dirt.

Don't suck your thumb, Donald. Did you hear what I read, Donald? His head was off, Donald! His head was gone! If you're going to wet your pants, Donald, do it in the hall. Hurry! Stella, Stella! Donald wet his pants again! You better not tell her we were in there, Donald, or someone might take your head off. What are you yelling about, Stupid?

I don't know what's wrong with him, Stella. What is it, honey?

Essy listens to the story about our father killing the German. I don't believe it, she says.

It's true, Essy, it's true, he wrote it, do you think our father lies? Are you saying he's a liar, Essy?

I've brought the page into our bedroom, I'm taking a chance my father's drunk. He's alone downstairs. It's a delicious game I'm playing.

25

You have to listen, Essy, or you can't come to the party.

What party? she sobs.   Any party, ever, I say.

Essy's having one of her fits, but no one cares. No one does a thing about it, no matter how loud she yells. Father's the only one at home and he's drunk, all right. I hear him winding the key on the bottom of the brown jug. We can hear it playing HOW DRY I AM   It sings, in a tiny, tinny voice, over and over,   Nobody knows how dry I am, nobody knows but Jesus, over and over, it sings the same words, and when it begins to run down, he winds it up again.

And before I could move,
I was buried by sandbags,
clay and dirt, and could
not move hand nor foot.
       Pte. M. G.

No head, Donald.

Blood on his hands, Essy.

"A face in the next bed beyond description." What do you think—maybe his nose was gone?

Buried Alive! He had dirt in his eyes, Donald. He couldn't move.

Donald and Essy begin to have nightmares. Father says that we can't listen to Chandu the Magician on the radio any more, it is too scary. I go up to my room and scream and scream until he relents, but just for me, because I'm the oldest.

When I begin to have nightmares, I blame Donald and Essy for making all that fuss. They are humble little people, and they believe what I say. They are to blame for everything.

My breathing became more
difficult, I was gradually
losing consciousness.
        Pte. M. G.

My father and Miranda and Aunt Emmy and Doctor and my great grandfather, the one Agnes loved so much, were all in the delivery room at the hospital when I was born. Agnes says this was because her grandfather was such an important man. Everyone loved him and so they let him do anything he wanted; he could park his car in a no-parking zone and say to the policeman, You watch that for me, my boy, and the policeman would salute and say, Don't you worry, Doctor. She says that my father should have been a doctor and he would have if it weren't for that war, he was already a pre-medical student at Alfred when the stupid thing broke out and Canada went in, and off he went to enlist. He didn't really have to go at all, but he was full of patriotic fervor—he was only a boy. It shouldn't be allowed, she says, the old men should be sent off to fight and that would be the end of the whole silly business. I say, like your grandfather?

She says, don't be an idiot. He always had more important things to do.

I sank into oblivion.
Pte. M. G.

The nuns are holding their black skirts up and running alongside the railroad track calling, Emily, Emily!

She's not Aunt Emmy yet, she's just the little Protestant child whose parents are at the end of their rope with her, the bad little girl with calluses on her knees from doing penance. She is riding away from the convent, away from the nuns on a railway handcar, dressed like a boy. She is as bad as a girl can be in those days and she will never stop no matter how long they call to her. She is sailing past the farmhouses and the churches, the white birches in the valleys and the scraggly pines on the stony hills, past the little ponds that shine back at the sun from the fields of Queen Anne's lace and blue Chicory. Now she is flying along the edge of the sea and the gulls are screaming Bad girl, bad girl, go, go, go! She is riding into another time, into the time of meeting Doctor and living in Blue Fields, Nicaragua and having Miranda and coming back here and working for the Draft Board and meeting Agnes and telling her about my father, as handsome as a movie star, which Agnes didn't believe until she saw the picture of him in uniform, and, lo, it was true, says Aunt Emmy, oh boys, was it true!

(Most people say Oh boy! Not Aunt Emmy. She always says boys. She eats in the English way with her fork upside down. I love to watch her. I love to listen to her. I love the way she handles a cigarette, carelessly, dropping the ash anywhere at all. She doesn't care. She is an Aristocrat, she says so herself.)

Well, it wasn't long until that child on the handcar was smoking and drinking champagne and dancing and everything that happened to her was like a movie. When she and Doctor eloped to Niagara Falls there were fields and fields of violets, as far as the eye could see from their hotel room window. I love the thrilling way she whispers,—Oh, those violets, darling, those violets! Doctor doesn't remember the violets, maybe he never noticed. Doctor doesn't smoke, it makes your lungs black, but Aunt Emmy doesn't care, she keeps the shades down all day on the damned sun (Sorry, darling!) and fills the living room with Pall Mall smoke. Her cigarettes are always broken because of the nail file she uses to open the packs, and while she talks she picks tobacco flakes off her lips. Oh darling, she cries, I don't know what I'd do without my bible and a cigarette once in a while!

There is a picture of my father in uniform in The Bulletin, along with his story of being buried alive. The same picture, larger and framed, is on the fireplace mantel in Aunt Emmy's living room next to the big curly seashell that contains the sound of waves. My young father stares through the drifting Pall Mall smoke. Seashells and buried-alive-by-a-German-shell and Blue Fields and battlefields mix pleasantly in the delicious sleepy afternoon cigarette smell. Dozing on the rug while Aunt

Emmy recalls those violets, I dream about the girl in the fairy tale whose words became flowers as they left her lips.

The heaviest load seemed
to be across my chest.
        Pte. M. G.

Aunt Emmy's life has been beautiful, darling, but also very difficult, and that part is thanks to Doctor's damned principles, (sorry, darling). The man wouldn't join the AMA, called them a bunch of crooks. Oh, he didn't say it that way, the silly man is polite to a fault, but those big doctors are not stupid, they knew what he meant, and even crooks have feelings, for heavens sake, well of course they kept him from getting into the best hospitals and he hasn't made any money from that day to this, but hi ho, darling, he's still my Romeo, so what's to do? Ah well, if it weren't for you, making sunshine when you come into the room...oh boys, when I think what we had in the tropics and now what we've come to, hunkered down in this upper flat under these nasty pinched ceilings like a couple of dogs in a kennel. What a setting for a Doctor's wife! Grubbing like a coolie in the kitchen. Paper curtains on the windows. Paper!

I stare at the big red roses printed all over the curtains. Some of the red is outside the lines, like the color in the Sunday funnies. The curtains belong to Miranda, and so does the house. I find it all quite wonderful, and, sweetly at peace, I doze in the hammocky rise and fall of the continuing music of Emmy's remarkable life. (Servants, a cook, anyone of any importance, oh boys! Those handsome naval officers, rice paddies, natives, stark naked, screamed and galloped away and so gentlemanly, not one of them said a word, then everything went straight to hell, excuse me, darling, silly revolution, natives always excited about something, very bad, oh, war is a terrible thing!)

Aunt Emmy can't stand Miranda's husband, Richard. Miranda was very beautiful when she was young. I can tell by her Memory Book, it's full of pressed corsages. Some are orchids! She could have done much better! She could have married anyone!

The effect of all these repeated words is that of light pouring in through cathedral windows. A respectful silence always follows. Miranda's daughter, my cousin Coletta, turns the pages of the memory book with trembling fingers. The faintly sweet odor of Miranda's yellowing past is almost unbearable.

Cheap, cheap! Aunt Emmy whispers whenever Richard appears. He pretends not to hear, but I know he does. Aunt Emmy tries to sound as if she is trying to sound like a canary. Richard is not fooled by this mixed message. He ought to be a handsome man, but he is very near to being a giant, and his proportions are off somehow. There is something horrible about this man who is a clerk in the office of a distant relative; it is as if he'd fooled Miranda into seeing him as handsome and then, once they were married, had taken off the disguise. There is a snapshot of him in her memory book, a profile of his head, which is beautiful. He teases me by tickling me and telling me I'm ugly. I try to stay away from him.

Miranda dances, naked, in the hall downstairs, in front of anyone. Only ignorant people are ashamed of their bodies, she says. Agnes agrees, but she sees no reason to demonstrate the fact in dance. The body is a wonderful machine and it is your duty to take care of the only one you are ever going to have. My mother dresses and undresses in her closet.

Miranda's hair is still very red and long. Agnes says that on the day of the Armistice, when all the bells began to ring, Miranda, who was in a beauty parlor at the time, ran out into the street with her hair streaming in the wind and a towel over her shoulders. She was having her hair hennaed, though no one was supposed to know.

It turned out to be true about the henna, you could tell when she got cancer. After she died, Richard said he was never going to marry again. He was saving himself for Miranda when he found her in heaven. Poor Miranda, said Agnes, she probably thought death was an escape.

Emmy had Picasso's eyes, not the color, the intensity. I recognized them years after her death, in a magazine photo. Emmy didn't paint, but she did make dents in the kitchen walls. Agnes pointed them out to me when Emmy had gone to the nursing home. Emmy made the dents, Agnes explained, by throwing pans at the walls.

Emmy's emotion recollected in my tranquility, she said, touching one of the indentations. Her statement surprised me. Agnes's life never became tranquil, as far as I could see.

I heard no sound
of the din above me,
yet the shells were
still bursting nearby.
            Pte. M. G.

Everything changes after Fifi Delsart shows up at the drama school with her spoiled little daughter Gigi and all those fancy clothes from Paris. Fifi Delsart was invented by my cousin Coletta who is not only Miranda's daughter but Aunt Emmy's granddaughter. She is almost three years older than I am and the whole city lies between our two houses, but we are best friends and for a while we exchange visits every weekend.

Coletta is very plain, poor child, says Agnes, It is killing Miranda—she has always been a jealous woman.

I don't look at Agnes. I'm ashamed that we're both happy that Coletta is plain and I'm not. I'm afraid that we'll exchange a smile and I am beginning to feel that I do not want anything like collusion with my mother in any area.

Coletta, who plans to be an artist, had drawn Fifi Delsart and painted her with water colors at about the same time she began talking about boys and wearing nail polish. The paper dolls stay at my house in a two-pound Whitman's candy box. Coletta and I had collaborated on the idea of the drama school, which was run by an old lady who looked like a schoolteacher. I had cut her out of a Sunday comic page. Her name is Mrs. Holiphant and she wears a pince-nez and a large bosom. She is very strict with the young ladies who attend school. Actually, things began to change even before Fifi arrived—it was Daphne Latimer, a younger, very pretty paper doll in scanty lace underwear, also invented by Coletta, who was suddenly one day the new director. Not only was the school now called the Daphne Latimer School of Drama, but, overnight it had moved to Paris, France. Mrs. Holiphant did not approve of the new pupils. They were unsuitable, she said. A lot of them had daring and vivacious personalities based on the various roles played by Jeanette MacDonald, who, along with Nelson Eddy, was the subject of elaborate scrapbooks kept by my cousin.

Mrs. Holiphant did not approve of men joining the school, among them Max Baer, the boxer, also clipped from the Sunday funnies. The students were housed in envelopes decorated on the outside to represent furnishings and artifacts appropriate to the personalities of their inhabitants. In a particularly daring move, Coletta slipped men into certain of the envelopes occupied by women. Their names began to appear on the envelopes next to those of the women. The first time she did it, Coletta looked at me with a sickly smile and blushed. Mrs. Holiphant, who had been offered the job of cook and had declined, had lately been existing in a sort of limbo at the bottom of the candy box. She now moved out. I felt sad about Mrs. Holiphant, whom I had rather liked, but I said nothing. Coletta's behavior, which suggested a superior knowledge of the ways of a world I had only glimpsed so far, impressed me.

One day, with a sly smirk, and no blushing, Coletta inserted a baby into one of the envelopes. Whose is it? I asked. Flossie's, said Coletta, and Max Baer's.

But they're not even married, I said.

Coletta, who had recently developed a laugh based on the musical one perfected by Jeanette MacDonald, covered her mouth with one of the hands Agnes once described as flaccid and useless-looking. I stared at the red polish. The hand was freckled, like Jeanette MacDonald. I raised my eyes and exchanged with Coletta what felt like the very look I'd refused my mother, and I began to laugh too. I was only fooling, I lied.

Agnes says that Coletta and I spend too much time imagining things. Get out in the fresh air, she orders, ride your bicycles. You'll ruin your eyes, she says, writing those tiny paper doll letters. Coletta is a bad influence, she complains, she is too dreamy, she is pale as a fish and you ought to encourage her to get out into the sun. But Agnes continues to let us get together on weekends. She even carries our big dolls back and forth on visits when she is going to see Aunt Emmy, and she mails our letters with the paper doll letters inside.

When I have to get glasses, though, she is very upset, and blames Coletta and the tiny letters. After that she makes me drink carrot juice and do boring eye exercises to strengthen the muscles. Glasses, says Agnes, are no more than a crutch. You can train your eyes to see without them. She herself has never needed glasses, and in fact, she says, has always seen far more than she cared to. I am not forbidden to write or read the tiny letters.

There are other new rules. When Coletta visits, we are required to play outside for two hours after breakfast and after lunch for three. Coletta really hates the arrangement. Sometimes I take her over to Gladys' and we play with the colorful gift-package ribbons manufactured by Gladys' father. Coletta can't stand her, but it isn't too bad if we can get Gladys to quit talking and laughing and sit instead at the breakfast nook table with us while we all write stories and draw cartoons. We can never be sure that Gladys won't get nasty and tear up all the stories and scribble on the drawings. That makes Coletta cry, even though she is older. Gladys turned Junior McShane's eyebrows permanently white by putting Saniflush on them—it's a lucky thing he can still see.

When Agnes says it's no wonder Gladys is crazy she means because of Gladys' father probably murdering his first wife, the one before Gladys' mother. Everyone is sure he did it. Agnes lets me play with Gladys because of being a good friend of Gladys' grandmother, who is worried to death about what will become of her granddaughter. That's what Agnes says. Worried to death.

When I come home from Gladys' Agnes always wants to know what happened there. Was her mother home? Was her father there? Was anyone else?

*It seemed ages before
I heard the heavenly sound
of a spade striking into
the dirt.*
                    Pte. M. G.

One day when Coletta is crying because of something Gladys did, I bring her home and try to make her feel better by taking her into the den and showing her what my father wrote about the war. I don't let her touch anything, but I read The Long Trail to her in a whisper because of Stella being downstairs.

Night was coming on, I read, *as we passed through a quiet village, and far away down the road we had come, the shadows were deepening, and I found myself humming the tune of THE LONG TRAIL.*

This was after my father was wounded at The Front, I say importantly, though I know she knows all about it. Coletta's father was never at The Front.

Aunt Emmy had told me that he managed to get out of it the way he got out of everything. He had flat feet, Aunt Emmy said, and the army didn't want him. He has more that's flat than that, she's willing to bet, she said to my mother. My mother frowned at her, but she was laughing too.

Who would want him anyway except Miranda, said Aunt Emmy, and even she has lived to regret the impulse or whatever you call it that got her into the whole mess in the first place. Watch out for men, she warned me, They'll be all over you one of these days.

Coletta is not crying any more but she looks very sad, as if she is thinking about her father and how the army didn't want him. She also notices the shadow of the lady next door on the green shade. Let's get out of here, she says, looking scared. I decide then and there to show her the gun in the drawer. Coletta looks and says it gives her the creeps. Don't touch it, she says.

You promised not to tell, I remind her. Coletta nods. Shut the drawer please, she says, let's go outside.

Some of the earth was
loosened about my head
and I could breathe
the air again.
            Pte. M. G.

Grandfather Gresham makes Agnes see red. Now retired and living by himself in Canada, he had been an Editor on the Herald Tribune (in New York City, he always adds.) His white mustache curls up at the ends in a way Agnes detests. He carries a cane with an ivory dog's head at the top and always holds himself so erect that you can't help noticing that he is putting a great deal of effort into the accomplishment.

He never says much to me or to Donald or Essy, except that we should stand straight, with our shoulders back and our heads up, like soldiers. We have never been kissed by him—they are alike in this—Agnes is not a kissing person either. Agnes does not wish to be touched, even by her children.

I often watch my grandfather from the windows of my room, which overlook the garden at the back of the house. I use the periscope Uncle Salmon and Aunt Sophie gave me for my birthday. My grandfather can stand for a very long time without moving. He stares at the yellow roses on the trellis that curves over facing seats, set too close for knee comfort. Even when he walks over to confront the lush peonies, he keeps his back straight and his head up. His imperious way with peonies never fails to impress me. He may lift his cane and point at a flower, not quite touching it, as if he is questioning it. Just once I saw him lift a red peony bloom with the tip of his cane. He leaned closer as if to carefully inspect its center. Astonishment opened in me as if I were the flower.

One of the things Agnes can't stand about him is the way he brags about his ancestors. He carries papers with him which prove that his family is not Irish, as some ignorant person once assumed, but English. He claims to be descended from William the Conqueror, and says that Essy and Donald and I ought to be very proud of this.

I have been told not to interrupt the conversations of adults, but I can't help myself. I say— Agnes is descended from him too!

I know this because she has told me so, only because she was explaining the awfulness of her grandmother, the snob, who paid someone to look up what Agnes calls that ancestor nonsense, so that she would be eligible to join the DAR. Agnes had vowed as a child that she would never descend to bragging about the past. She says that the present is all that matters and it is up to each of us to make our own good history.

Does being related to William the Conqueror that way mean that we are all cousins then, besides everything else? I persist.

No, says Agnes, it does not. She says this in her tight voice, the one she uses when Grandfather Gresham is in town. She tells me to go to my room and do my homework. I listen through the floor register and am surprised to hear Agnes bragging about her ancestors in just the way she claims her grandmother did.

Agnes can't stand Aunt Regina either. She's my father's older sister and an old maid teacher of history in a private school in New York City. I listen through the open window from Gladys' grandmother's garden as Agnes tells her that it was Regina who encouraged my father to drink, out of jealousy—she always resented him, she is a selfish, bitter person, Agnes says. Gladys sees me listening there and comes over from chipping paint off one of the garden gnomes. She hears Agnes say that the reason my Grandmother Gresham had only two children was because she didn't want any more and would get an abortion whenever she got pregnant, which was often, because of my grandfather being a sex fiend. She was able to get the abortions because of knowing so many doctors in New York City. She died from cancer of the breast, which was probably a direct result of all those abortions. And that, says Agnes, is the family that old goat is so stuck up about!

Gladys tells me what abortion means. What? I say. I don't believe it! Then she tells me about babies and how they get inside the mothers' stomachs in the first place.

That's terrible! I say. Gladys laughs. She never seems to think that anything is terrible.

She also tells me about sex fiends, but I don't believe her. Everybody knows that Gladys is a liar.

Imagine my horror
when I heard one of
the diggers say, "It's
no use, Bert, he's dead."
      Pte. M. G.

Gladys says she's bored. It's the fourth of July and she has red and blue polish on her toenails and fingernails. We're all at her house on one of the tennis courts at the back and my father is going to light the big gas balloon. It's safer to do it here than at home because there are fewer houses for the balloon to fall on and burn the roof the way it did last year on the Jordans'. But Agnes says you never know with a thing like that, where it's going to land for lord's sake, and she doesn't want anything to do with it, so she stays inside with Gladys' mother drinking the sherry Gladys' father smuggled over from Canada.

The little kids' faces are red with excitement. They're all yelling and tugging at Stella. The littlest Jordan girl has wet her pants. There's a big stain on the seat of her sun suit and her father wants to get a picture of her like that. Now she's sitting on the grass sucking her thumb and screaming with her eyes closed. Stella is kneeling next to her, talking quietly. Firecrackers are going off all over town. It sounds like a battlefield—that's what Agnes always says. It's a wonder to her that my father can stand it after all he went through.

Gladys sits next to me in the grass and yawns. She says, You want to use my nail polish?

I nod.

The blue too? I ask.

Sure.

Where did you get them? I ask.

She says, from the five and ten. I stole them.

I don't believe you. She shrugs.

Well, can I use them? I ask.

I already said you could, only, not here. Let's go over to your house. There's no one around there.

Oh yes, there is too, I say, my grandfather's there.

Your grandfather! she says, he's deaf, he'll never notice. Come on, if you want to use the polish. Besides, I know something that's at your house I bet you don't even know about.

What, Gladys? What do you mean? I say.

Never mind, she says, I won't tell you unless we go over there. So come on.

We go in the side door, down to the cellar. Gladys says the thing she means is in the fruit cellar. This is where Stella keeps the glass jars of chili and pineapple conserve and peaches and watermelon pickles. Gladys reaches back of the conserve and brings out a bottle. See? she says, It's your father's whisky.

How did you know it was there? I ask, and Gladys says, They all keep them in the cellar.

I say, Why? And Gladys says, To hide them from their nosy wives, and I say, Agnes isn't nosy.

And Gladys says, They all are, have a swig, and she takes a drink right from the bottle and hands it to me.

You promised I could use the polish, I say, and Gladys says, After we have a little more, and I shake my head and Gladys says, You're scared of a little bottle in your own house, and I say, I am not, and Gladys says, You are too, and I take a drink and it's awful. I want to spit it out, but I swallow it. Gladys laughs and has some more and then I have some more and it's not so bad this time and I notice how beautiful the jars are in the sun that comes in through the little high window; the colors of the jams and the jellies and the preserved peaches and the conserve spill on the floor and dance along the walls and the cobwebs are silver. I think of the story of the twelve princesses who danced underground all night every night and brought back a silver branch from a tree that made their father suspicious, and I feel very sleepy and a little scared.

After a while we are in my room, looking through the periscope at my grandfather standing in the garden with his back to us, staring at the iris bed. He bends over to pick one of the blooms and puts the flower in his buttonhole. Gladys giggles. Shut up! I say, he'll hear you!

He can't even hear the fireworks, stupid, Gladys says, and giggles harder.

I feel sick. I run into the bathroom and when I come out again into the hall, Gladys is just leaving my parents' room. I went to look for cigarettes, she says, and look what I found! She brings her hand out from behind her back. The gun points straight at me. I yell—You put that back! You put that back! and Gladys laughs and sticks her tongue out and pushes past me into my room. She points the gun out the window at my grandfather's back. Don't! I yell, don't, don't, don't! Grandpa, watch out! I shout, help! But he doesn't hear me. He looks like a dollhouse doll down there, like the little china prince with jointed arms and legs, the one Coletta made the black velvet suit with the lace collar for. My grandfather's cane looks like the prince's sword that's really a pin.

Sex fiend! Gladys is yelling. The sound the gun makes is terrible, even with all the firecracker noise. I scream and scream and still I hear that explosion. The walls are rocking with it. Gladys is sitting on the floor, looking scared. There is a white line all around her mouth.

When I look again, my grandfather is still standing there looking at the iris bed.

The gun is on the floor. I take it and put it back into the drawer in my parents' room. Gladys is laughing when I get back. I hit her just as the big gas balloon shows in the sky, shooting flames. I hit her again, harder. Gladys looks surprised. Tears fill her eyes. Her nose is bleeding. She begins to whimper. I want to hurt her as much as I can, but just then the back door opens and my grandfather shouts—Anybody home?

I yell at Gladys, Get out! And she does, stumbling down the stairs and out the front door with her hand to her nose. In the back hallway, I throw myself into my grandfather's arms. Well now, he says, well now—scared of the fireworks, are you, little girl? And he pats me on the back and extricates himself.

Just like my little sister, he says, Girl used to hide under the bed with the cats. Say, I bet this'll cheer you up, he says, and shows me his cane. The dog's head is gone.

Darndest thing! he says, That ivory dog on my cane just blew up, shattered to bits out there all of a sudden. Darndest thing—might be the heat did it. You live long enough, Martha, you could see everything. It's a remarkable world.   It's the most he's ever said to me.

That night in bed I cry with rage when I remember that Gladys never let me use the blue nail polish.

Then I gathered all my
forces and tried to shout.
       Pte. M. G.

Agnes was afraid that Sophie, her younger brother Salmon's wife, would appear at our house while Grandfather Gresham was visiting. This was possible. Sophie was given to dropping in without calling first, another proof that she was irretrievably Ukrainian or something; whatever it was, a group incapable of planning ahead. Other national, possibly racial traits—poor English, a loud voice, lots of makeup, tatting in vulgar colors. Sophie gave gift handkerchiefs with tatted edges. Agnes put them out of sight as soon as possible.

Nevertheless, she was the only one in the family who was nice to Salmon and Sophie. Flavius Josephus wouldn't speak to either of them and neither would his wife Charlotte. Of course Charlotte never spoke to anyone. Agnes said this was because she was not very bright and had nothing to say. Even so, Charlotte's polite detached smile and her expensive, simply cut oatmeal-colored dresses maddened Agnes.

Charlotte's one activity was serving on the Board of the art gallery in the city. That woman, said Agnes, hangs around that gallery as if she thinks talent is catching. Someone ought to explain to her that she's immune.

Sophie and Salmon were invited almost every weekend for Sunday dinner because Agnes felt sorry for Salmon, who was the baby of the family. She had fed and diapered him, thanks to her mother's famous incompetence. One of Agnes's (self-imposed) duties had been to walk him around the block in a wicker baby carriage. This very carriage was depicted in our book of family snapshots, with tiny Uncle Salmon inside and my straight-backed mother looking coolly at the camera as if it had challenged her to behave with dignity. It was, eerily, Agnes's face I saw there, except that it was attached to the body of a girl younger than myself.

As the door closed behind Sophie and Salmon on Sunday evenings, Agnes could usually be counted upon to remark that her mother ought to have had that marriage annulled right away. Agnes and Flavius had told her so, but of course the woman never did a thing about it. She even let the two of them move in with her for a while. And now of course it was too late, because even though Salmon certainly saw by now (you could tell by his embarrassment at the way she carried on) how he'd ruined his life, Sophie and that family of hers would never let him go. Why, poor Salmon was only 16—16! And Sophie was 18 and you know how it is with girls of that sort, they grow up very fast, much faster than we do!

That awful family of hers! They thought they were moving up in the world. Sophie's mother actually tried to tip my grandfather after he examined her—he only agreed to do it because Sophie begged him to. He would never say no, such a gentleman—I wish you children could have known him—and never in his life sent out a bill. He always said that anyone who could afford to would pay. Sophie's mother gave him a dollar extra. She slipped it into his pocket and patted it and said, That's for you, Doctor.

And what do you think my grandfather did, children? Agnes would ask. That's right, Essy, he thanked her, he was such a gentleman. He knew how to behave. But it was lost on that crew, all right.

I loved Sophie and Salmon. Sophie kissed me and hugged me a lot and told me I was beautiful. I even liked the handkerchiefs with the tatted edges, though I kept this evidence of inferior taste to myself. Agnes said that whole crew, by which she meant Sophie's family, were forever kissing and hugging. It was certainly easier for them than intelligent conversation, she said.

Although the official view was that their marriage was a disaster, Sophie and Salmon seemed to be in love. They even appeared to like one another. They always sat close together on the davenport and laughed a lot. It may be funny to them, said Agnes, but it's no joke to the rest of the family. This observation was often followed by the story of how my grandmother had allowed those two to stay with her even after Sophie embarrassed her to death by leaning out the upstairs window so that her bare breasts showed and yelling down at the moving men when they brought in the furniture. Of course, said Agnes, Your grandmother never took an independent step in her entire career—it was easier to let them stay than to confront them. Agnes's worst insult, when she was really mad at me, was that I was just like my grandmother. Actually, I liked Grandma, whose clothing was sometimes held together with safety pins, whose hair was always working its way out of its careless mooring at the back of her neck, so that a strand of it hung over her face. She reminded me of the White Queen in Alice. She made angora hats for my dolls and spoke in a genteel whisper. Agnes laughed at the hats. She said they were made almost entirely of dropped stitches.

They continued their efforts,
and soon I was out up to my waist.
    Pte. M. G.

Donald and Essy and I are in our parents' room. So is Stella. She has brought us here by way of the back stairs. Stella tells us to hide under the beds and stay quiet. I slide under my father's bed. Essy, who is already under Agnes's, next to Donald, moves over next to me. She is trembling. Donald moves over too. He has wet his pants and smells terrible. I tell them to go back where they were. Shhh! Stella warns. We all freeze.

I dare after a while to raise my head. I dare to pull myself a little out from under the bed. Stella's back is to us. Her hair, in the blaze of winter light, looks polished. Her slender hand shows clear against the white window frame. Stella is looking out the window, but she is trying not to be seen from outside. Very quietly, I inch forward until I can kneel. I look past Stella down to the street. A black automobile is parked there in the snow, trapped between two Venetian blind slats.

A tall man in a black coat gets out of the automobile. He comes up the sidewalk toward the house, appearing in sections between the slats. His face flicks on and off as if he's in a movie with projector trouble, like the one my father borrows from Gladys' father to show our home movies. The man stops and raises his head to look at the house. He seems to be looking directly at me. I stare back until he disappears.

The brass knocker strikes the front door. The floor shivers. The perfume bottles and windowpanes ring. Stella is shaking all over. She looks like Rapunzel with that long golden hair of hers. The knocker hits the door again and again. The doorbell rings, again and again. Now the man is banging with his fist or maybe something even harder. Stella's shoulders are hunched. She is hugging herself tight. When she turns her head, I can see that her lips are moving. Maybe she is praying. Donald whimpers.

She turns with a finger to her lips as the man's footsteps sound on the wooden porch stairs. She does not seem to see me kneeling there on the Numdah rug. She turns back again as the man appears on the sidewalk. He makes no sound. It is as if he floats back to his automobile.

I am suddenly afraid that when Stella opens the door to the upstairs hall, there will be a motorcycle out there. It doesn't happen. The idea comes from one of my worst nightmares, in which a roaring motorcycle does come into the house, up the stairs to the hall, to the very door of my bedroom. Each time, I wake just before it can come in.

As I follow Stella down the stairs, I feel a strange calmness growing with each step we take. The front door is calm, so are the tall windows in the living room that look out into the empty street. But it is as if they are pretending that eerie calm in order to hide something. I am frightened now of everything, of the player piano, the oatmeal colored wallpaper, the davenport (oatmeal also), and particularly of the machine-stitched tapestry hanging over the davenport depicting elegant old-fashioned people in an elegant old-fashioned room. An edge of the oriental carpet on which they stand is wrinkled, a realistic effect over which my mother and her friends often exclaim. The humped-up portion of rug, its stitches further depicted in the stitches of the tapestry, now seems to possess the sinister glow of the impossible idea of eternity.

The familiar chairs too are ominous, so are the tables and the lamps. We follow Stella over the oriental rug, past the gray cat curled on the hearth. The French doors to the summer parlor, next to the wall of books, are locked for the winter, but I can see a section of the parlor—the edge of a grass rug, the arm of the wicker rocker, and on a round table, a tray of lemonade glasses— all of it blurred by the lace curtains on the French doors. Snow is falling past the wide summer windows behind the leaf-green glasses. A book whose title I cannot see lies face down on the grass rug.

The dining room is horrible. It is filled today with the dead feeling of the very worst Sundays, its furniture heavy as the smell of roasting meat filling the closed winter house. Essy and Donald and me on our stomachs on the floor reading the comic pages on the funny-paper-colored rug, all of us yawning with nervousness, the house too hot. And all day long, the sound of Father's typewriter issues from his den like a crackle of fire. Our father is not home yet, and it is not Sunday, but the day's personality has somehow established itself in this room and will not go away.

In the kitchen, Stella finishes the three-layer cake for my birthday. Roses, birds, curly leaves emerge from the paper cone Stella squeezes along the sides and the top of the enormous cake. Stella's hands are sure, steady.

I ask my father about the dark man and the automobile, but it is Agnes who laughs and says that Stella must owe someone money again.

I don't believe her. I look at my father, but he just nods and smiles.

Happy birthday, says Agnes. She turns off the dining room lights and Stella brings in the cake while they all sing. I blow out the candles.

When Stella is out of the room, Agnes laughs and says she wonders why Stella's productions always look like wedding cakes. She looks at the cake as if it is one of Sophie's hankies.

A peculiar droning hum.
Pte. M. G.

Honk honk honk.

Oh, for lord's sake, says Agnes, oh my god! MARTHA! You go keep him in the back yard, oh why did they have to choose today of all days! Thank god he's deaf.

That's not nice. I say.

Don't be fresh! Just keep him out of here. I'll get rid of Sophie somehow.

Are you ashamed of Sophie?

I'm not ashamed of anyone except a daughter who can't keep a civil tongue in her head. Now you get out of here, young lady, and do what I say or I'll give you a taste of not nice! Go on, right now! Keep your grandfather entertained.

But I'm hypnotized by Sophie's brand new red roadster convertible, and by Sophie coming up the front walk calling, Yoohoo, anyone home? The lady next door is walking her dog; she crosses the street and pretends not to notice anything, in such a way that there is no question that she is taking in every embarrassing detail. The bridge club that Agnes refuses to join because it's common and a waste of time, is meeting across the street at the Donaldsons'. Curtains are drawn back and they all peek out at Sophie and her sister and mother, large women, all of them, with hearty voices. Sophie's mother's hair is the color of Jean Harlow's. They are all teetering on thin high heels that are also red. Sophie is crying out that they went downtown and bought shoes to match the roadster Salmon gave her for her birthday. She shouts that she has attached sleigh bells to the car.

Come for a ride! She calls to the house, to the neighborhood.

I'm ordering you, young lady! Get out there!

Don't pinch me! She did once, and I don't let her forget it.

Get out!

Agnes went for a ride with them. She rode in the rumble seat! She claimed she was on her way to visit Mrs. Dee, and she had them drop her off there. Agnes went for a ride in that wonderful car and didn't even enjoy it! I would have loved it. I would have adored being tucked in among those soft women who smelled of powder and perfume and sachet and who probably wore black lace underwear, not sensible cotton like Agnes.

Instead, I stood in the backyard with my grandfather, staring at the marigolds that smelled musty, like old men. I heard all that excitement, all that laughing and shouting, and I heard the car start up and zoom off and I imagined that red streaking down the middle of our oatmeal colored street and I wanted to hit Agnes.

When she got back, she said it was the worst day of her life. I said, You're a mean old snob, just like your grandmother! She sent me to my room. At least you didn't pinch me this time, I said, as I started up the stairs. She threw a book at me.

I twisted around so as to
face the German trenches,
for I knew they would be
charging now.
        Pte. M. G.

Agnes says that even her own mother noticed something about Flavius years ago. Even my own mother, she says, who never noticed anything unpleasant if she could avoid it. Agnes says,   Flavius was always jealous of me, of course. Maybe that has something to do with it, she says.

My father says,   Little pitchers.

Agnes says,   Go to bed right now, right this minute, young lady, scat!

I knew what she was going to say anyway, that Uncle Flavius thought she got to live with her grandfather because she was a girl. But did she want to? Did she have any choice? Then she would say that the truth was her mother didn't care a scrap for her. Flavius was still jealous to this day. She would say it as if it made her happy, even though you were supposed to think it didn't.

Gladys says Uncle Flavius is a fairy. She tells me what it means.   I don't believe her.   What about Charlotte?   I say, she's his wife.   Gladys laughs at me. But she's the only one I tell about what really happened in my grandmother's garden. That was the day Sophie hit Flavius. I watched from the Indian cave in the field back of the garden. So did my grandmother. I saw her face at her kitchen window. Flavius came into the garden where Sophie was bent over, doing some weeding. She stopped by every week to help my grandmother. It was nice of her, Agnes always said, but you could tell by the way she said it that she didn't like it.

Flavius touched Sophie on her behind. I saw him do it, but the light was so funny, it was hard to be sure. I was in the cave looking for arrowheads and I found one just when he did it and she stood up and he grabbed her around the waist and tried to kiss her, and she hit him right in the face. It was too bad she had the trowel in her hand, but it only cut him a little on the cheek. She was sorry afterward. I saw it all, only the light was funny, I was just coming out of the dark cave and it was starting to rain and it was hard to see anyhow through all the grape vines and the ivy my grandmother let grow over everything. So I never said. I never told what happened and neither did my grandmother. Well, maybe she couldn't see too well either, she was old and her eyes weren't so good—she was always losing her glasses, but I think she had them on. I think I noticed the flash of them, but I couldn't be sure. So I guess both of us just let Agnes say what she said, that Sophie was lying, that Flavius wouldn't behave that way and the best you could say about Sophie was she got it wrong the way her mother did when she tipped my great grandfather. And maybe that was the way it was. I couldn't tell for sure, could I? And I didn't say anything either when Sophie yelled at Salmon because he wouldn't stand up for her, she said. She said he was scared of his whole damn family. She said damn in front of Essy and me. Agnes said it was no wonder Essy talked the way she did with an influence like that in the family.

Gladys said that what happened in the garden didn't prove anything. Sometimes fairies do things like that, she said, just to make people think they're like everyone else.

"God! What a night!"
Pte. M. G.

I say, You said Charlotte has a mustache.

Agnes says she never said any such thing.

I say, Yes you did, you said so.

Well maybe I did, she says, but you weren't supposed to be listening. And don't repeat it, for heavens sake. It doesn't matter. Lots of people have mustaches.

Not ladies, I say. Agnes shrugs.

Does she shave in the morning? I ask. Agnes begins to giggle. She says she is going to wet her pants if I don't stop. She runs out of the room.

Agnes says, Who? Your uncle? That's ridiculous.

I say, He did so, Uncle Flavius tried on your hat. He sat there at your dressing table.

Agnes says, That's ridiculous. You were delirious. Don't bother me with your nonsense.

I say, It's not nice to lie to your own daughter.

She says she's sorry she was so nice to me that day because I was feverish and she let me stay in her bed and she read The Wind in the Willows to me when she could have been doing a hundred other things.

I say,   That's when he came in, when you fell asleep and the book slid off your lap onto the floor.

Alright, she says. He did come in. I forgot, it was so unimportant. But don't go telling people he tried on my hat and don't tell them about the lipstick. We were being silly; we used to play like that when I was your age, that's all.

I don't tell her he looked better than she did in the hat. Even when he stuck his tongue out at her when she wouldn't let him use her mascara.

And regular with steady
drum came the sputtering
of our machine guns and the
crack of our rifles.
            Pte. M. G.

Uncle Flavius said this whole town was one big harem. He said all the men drove off in the morning and turned into one big man in the city. He said it when he drank too much bathtub gin. That's what Agnes said. He said all the girls in the harem knew how to get along except for Gladys' mother. He said she didn't play the game. I asked Agnes what game and she said tennis, and to mind my own business.

Uncle Flavius said, You girls will get her someday. Agnes said, That's ridiculous. He meant Gladys' mother. He called her Gorgeous Milly.

I watch my father drive off to work. It is so sunny that by the time he reaches the corner, I'm not sure I can see his car anymore in all that moving, changing light. Maybe Flavius is right. Maybe it's at that corner the fathers begin to turn into one man. But I know it's not really true, because whenever I visit him at his office on the seventh floor of the Brattle Building, there he is, looking just the way he always does, smoking his pipe and smiling. His secretary Nora gives me peanuts to throw to the pigeons on the wide stone windowsills and lets me slide on the shiny marble floor of the long hall outside the office. I peek in to be sure he still looks like himself. He does, even against the light from the big window behind him. He is still my father and there is no one who looks better than he does. Even Nora thinks so. I can tell. She says she came to work here the day she got out of high school and she intends to stay forever. She tells me one day that the man selling apples on the street in front of the building is a doctor. Why is he selling apples, I want to know. The Depression, she says.

I love the sound of the tennis balls from the court behind the Dugans' garden next door. The mothers are polite. Sorry, partner, they call, and they shake hands afterward. I try to imitate that when I play with Gladys, but she gets mad if she loses and she throws her racket down and pushes me. Sometimes, though, it is wonderful. We play until it is too dark to see. The ball then is a little moon we keep hitting back and forth and sometimes it seems as if neither of us will ever miss a shot, and the air is like silk. In bed at night, the slow sweet arc of that ball keeps moving over my closed lids. But it is best I think to be at home listening to the thunk of the balls as the afternoon wears away. Stella closes the Venetian blinds in my parents' room and after a while the sounds from the court stop and Agnes comes home to nap before her bath. That is a lovely time too. The house is like the castle in The Sleeping Beauty. It is so silent that I tell myself I can hear the bushes growing outside. Years and years are passing and everyone is asleep. Even Stella is sitting quietly at the kitchen table, yawning and playing solitaire while a chocolate cake bakes in the oven. Snap! That must be the sound of a thorn breaking through on a branch that pushes at the window now. If Agnes does not wake up soon, no one will be able to get through those bushes. I am supposed to be resting, but I am not tired.

Agnes wakes and comes into the hall in an ivory satin slip. Her hair hangs down her back. She looks beautiful, like a princess in a fairy tale. She goes into the bathroom and turns on the water. The smell of her pine bath salts fills the hall. When she comes downstairs she is wearing high heels and a pretty dress and lipstick and she smells good and my father is coming in the front door and she kisses him and upstairs in her bedroom the perfume bottles are still jittering and making tiny ringing sounds on her dressing table. I feel happy, almost as if I am dreaming my favorite dream, the one in which I fly around the ceiling of the living room and everyone looks up at me and says Ooooooooh, the way they do when the gas balloon goes up on the fourth of July.

Don't ask so many questions, Agnes says, and what do you know about harems anyway?

I read about them at Mrs. Dee's, I say, and they're not one bit like this.

Agnes looks like the lady in the picture by Renoir in the downstairs hall when she sits in the lamplight with Donald in her lap. This is another time she's going to yell at me to get to bed and stop listening. I can tell. She wants to know what Gladys' mother was doing at my father's office. She calls her *Mil*dred. My father says she came in to change her policy and Agnes says, Not much chance of that—we all know what Mildred's policy is, if you can call it that, and my father says, Little pitchers, but she's too mad to listen, and she says, If you take her to lunch again, just don't drink. Just don't, she says, okay?

My father doesn't answer. Then Agnes yells, What are you doing, sneaking around down here—get to bed, young lady, this minute! She's mad at me because my father won't answer her! Also, she wakes Donald up with her yelling and he begins to cry, and it's no wonder—the poor thing has a terrible cold.

*My rescuers finished their job
and I was able to grasp a rifle and
assist in the mowing down of those
advancing hordes.*
  Pte. M. G.

That summer Agnes made a big mistake. She left Grandpa Gresham alone in the house for a whole day while we all went to a lecture by a cousin on her side of the family who taught mathematics in a college in a town about sixty miles away. It was a very dull lecture. Not one of us understood what it was about and my father fell asleep until Agnes noticed and nudged him. Donald wet his pants and began to cry and Agnes said she was mortified.

It was well after eleven by the time we got home that night, and Donald and Essy, who were sleeping, had to be carried in. I had never been up so late in my life and I was determined not to sleep, but to notice everything I could about the way things were in the dark of the night.

We found Grandfather Gresham drunk. We knew it when he opened the door and kissed us all. Donald and Essy woke up and began to sob. Agnes took them up to bed. When she came down again, Grandfather Gresham was in the middle of his story. He seemed delighted to start over again. He said that Sophie had come to visit with her mother and two sisters and a cousin.

Oh no! Agnes whispered, and sat down on the couch. She looked, to my surprise, very young, like Essy.

Her lips were trembling and she seemed to be struggling not to cry. It had been a difficult day altogether. She felt we had been snubbed by her cousin, who seemed vague about who we were and persisted in not understanding why we had attended a lecture directed at a professional audience. Agnes was reduced to saying that she thought he might enjoy having family there on his big day. He looked with some distaste at Donald, who smelled rancid. Well, thank you for coming, he said, and moved on to someone else. Why did I say that? Agnes mourned to my father. It wasn't what I meant, she said, I sounded like some idiot in that silly bridge club.

Don't worry about it, my father said, we've had a nice outing.

No we haven't, she said.

Agnes, sitting tiredly on the couch, looked warily at my grandfather. She must have wondered if he could be making fun of her. She'd spent years worrying about an encounter that had happened while she was not around to control its outcome, and it appeared that Grandfather Gresham had been impressed—impressed!—by Sophie and her crew. Agnes straightened her back and smoothed her hair.

There was, for me, something magic about being up at that hour. When midnight struck we all sat as if enchanted, while the fussy clock on the mantel (won by my father for selling more insurance than anyone else in the country) went through its Westminster repertoire.

After that was over, the events of the rest of that night began to possess the strange logic of a dream—for instance, there was the cousin theme. We had gone to see a cousin in another city and now found that another cousin had visited here. I thought it was quite wonderful—it was as if our trip had been one of those mathematical equations the other cousin had chalked on a freestanding blackboard. But this cousin of Sophie's was nothing like that dry little stick who had even made Agnes yawn. This one, according to my grandfather, was beautiful, this one was, amazingly, visiting from Yugoslavia, and looked like a queen, in a paisley shawl and gold hoop earrings.

Gypsies, Agnes mouthed.

Because my grandfather was deaf, he shouted all this information. Essy and Donald woke and cried and were brought down. Grandfather repeated what he had told us while Agnes was upstairs. That the mysterious cousin was an opera singer in Yugoslavia, a very famous one, he said, who had stopped only for a short visit and was going on to perform in New York City at the Metropolitan Opera House. I have been there many times, said Grandfather, in my youth.

He stumbled over a footstool as he rose to demonstrate where she had sat. Here, he said, on this very bench at this gimcrack piano, with her pretty feet on this rug, and she sang, oh how she sang—the Habenara from Carmen, and Mozart—The Magic Flute—if you had

73

only been here—these poor walls have never heard the like and never will again. She was a princess, I tell you.

Demoted, mouthed Agnes, She was a Queen a few blatherings back.

What cultivation, said Grandfather, what grace, wasting her sweetness on this desert air—that whole family comes from a larger world than any of us has ever known.

Drunk, said Agnes. The old fool's blotto.

Why are you crying, Martha? said my father.

I wish I stayed home. I want to hear her sing! I wailed.

You'd have heard nothing, believe me, but the sound of liquid moving from bottle to glass, said Agnes. It's all fantasy, every bit of it. He's making fun of me, that's what the old goat's doing.

Shut up, Agnes, said my father. You've gone too far.

Essy said, Father said a bad word! She began to sob.

Shut up, Essy, said Agnes, and took her into her lap.

Grandpa was leading us all out to the kitchen. Slibovitz, he said, holding up an empty bottle with some reverence. It was a large green one with a heavily embossed red and gold label, which I found very beautiful.

What is it? I asked.

Plum brandy, my dear, of exquisite quality. We drank it here, at this humble kitchen table. See these crumbs? Torte crumbs. He told me what a torte was, the most delicious, most sophisticated of cakes, a medley of subtle sweetnesses, the master baker's aria, he said.

I tasted a crumb. I licked the sticky sweetness on the edge of a brandy glass. Agnes yanked it away. Enough drunks in this family, she said. My father left the room, taking Essy and Donald with him. Agnes ran out after them. He's deaf, she was saying, how could he hear anyone sing?

I believe him, said my father. It was the last I saw of them until breakfast.

Grandpa seemed not to notice they were gone. He was going on and on about the lights in her curly black hair. From one crumb of torte, from one taste of Slibovitz, he cried, I offer you a world, little girl! He almost sang it. I tell you, little Martha, that woman blessed this house. In here, he said, pushing a section of the evening paper across the table. He tapped the paper with a trembling finger. There was indeed a picture of the woman he'd described, a Yugoslavian singer, briefly in town on her way to sing at the Metropolitan; all of it was there, just as he'd said. I was disappointed to find nothing about Sophie.

Poor Salmon, said my grandfather, as if he'd read my thoughts, he'll never be able to hang onto that girl. Doesn't have the balls, he confided. And then he fell asleep at the kitchen table, head in his arms.

I didn't want this night to end. I felt pure and direct as a line of light. I could smell the breath of old breakfasts, I could feel the absolute coldness of the porcelain-topped table. I pressed my hand on it and took in the idea of cold and hardness as if they were parts of a mathematical equation.

I looked at the long hairs moving in my grandfather's nostrils. I stared and stared. What did he mean by a larger world?

The shouts of the Germans...
       Pte. M. G.

If it bothers you so, ask Salmon.

Agnes stared at my father.   You know Salmon, you know how sensitive he is about her.

You don't have to say anything against her, for god's sake! Say you saw the article in the paper. Say you thought Sophie might be interested since the woman's from Yugoslavia.

Oh, I don't know. Sophie will call. Leave it to her, she'll want to brag. That's if it's true, which I'm convinced it's not. I'm sorry, I just know he's lying, that's all. He got it all from that newspaper article.

Well, the old man has been known to embroider the truth from time to time, but usually in a good cause.

Lying is lying.

You're a hard one, Agnes.

After a few days, Agnes couldn't stand the suspense. She called Salmon. She looked stunned when she came back to the kitchen where my father and I were doing the dishes on Stella's night off.

What's the matter, Ag?

I can't believe it. Salmon was crying, like a baby. Agnes herself began to cry. She stood there staring straight ahead, tears running down her cheeks. She didn't bother to wipe them away.   Poor Salmon. Oh poor Salmon. Such a hard life, she whispered.

My father put an arm around her and guided her to a chair.

She left him, said Agnes.   Sophie went off and left Salmon. Her whole family has left town, bag and baggage. Agnes began to sob. Oh, Salmon, she cried, how could they do that to you? How could she leave him? I don't understand anything anymore.

When my grandfather got the news, he said he wasn't surprised.

She went off with that opera singer, she went back to her own world, a larger world, Martha, a finer people than you've ever known, little girl, a singing people, a noble people!

He's drunk again.

Flavius has a black eye. He's not appearing in public until it's healed. Salmon gave it to him. That's the end, says Flavius, I tried to reach out to him in his time of need.

Flavius should have known better than to make remarks like that about Sophie to Salmon, says Agnes.

Yes, especially of the running off with the grocery delivery boy variety, says my father.

Agnes was taking a sensible view of things now. She said, Salmon is still young. It's a blessing in disguise and he'll see it that way someday.

I hate you! I said to Agnes. I cried, with my head on the piano bench where Sophie's beautiful cousin had sat. I cried and cried. I love Sophie, I want her to come back.

Well, she won't, said Agnes, so you'd better get used to the idea.

Grandfather Gresham didn't come back either. He died that year in Canada.

Agnes continued to say that the opera singer cousin was imaginary. Salmon moved to Los Angeles where he drove a taxicab for years. He never would say a word about any of it.

I hated Agnes's feet, the way they looked at the beach, and in her slippers, the toes white as garden slugs, squished together from wearing shoes that were too narrow, she says, when she was growing up. She blames her mother, who didn't notice things of that sort. Her grandmother didn't either, but that was because she was so jealous of Agnes that she couldn't bear to buy anything for her. Her grandfather had so many responsibilities and yet he was the one who noticed that her shoes were too small and took her to get new ones, but it was too late by then, the damage was done.

I don't want anyone else to see those crooked ugly toes of hers. They have taken on horrible shapes from being pressed against each other, there has never been enough room for them to grow they way they were meant to, like mine, separate, springy, as if each has a life of its own. I am afraid that mine will look like hers someday.

But this is even worse—I am also sorry for her toes, I am sorry that I know about them. I don't like her hands either, they are too wide, the fingers are short and the nails have no moons. She could cover them with red polish and no one would know. But she doesn't. She buffs her nails with a chamois brush and a powder to make them shine. She puts white under the tops of them. But this does not help. Why do they have no moons? Mine are like that too and I am ashamed of them. I think that they are little signs that something is wrong with this family. No matter how hard I push at my cuticle with an orangewood stick, there are no moons. Gladys has moons, big triumphant ones, and long slender fingers. Her grandmother's hands look like hers and she says that Gladys has musician's hands and Mrs. Dee pays for her piano lessons, but Gladys won't practice. I play better than she does with my short stubby fingers, but Gladys doesn't care. Essy has hands like mine and I hate to look at them. They make me feel like crying. She might as well be naked. You can tell everything about her from those hands. She just lets them hang there, as if she's some sort of ignorant creature from the ocean, a starfish we saw lying on the shore at Cape Cod looking disgusting—Essy won't even have the sense to put polish on them the way I will when I grow up. You can tell by looking at Essy's hands that people will not be nice to her when she grows up. You can tell that she will have a sad, horrible life.

I was dimly conscious of
a frightful pain across
my chest.
　　　Pte. M.G.

When I open the drawer, the papers stir. They make a whispery sound, as if they are saying the words printed on them. What if they begin to talk louder? What if they shout, I PLUNGED MY BAYONET INTO HIS BODY?

I shut the drawer. I hold it closed with the palms of my hands. I press hard, as if it might otherwise open by itself. My head aches. My stomach hurts the way it does when I have been running for a long time. I remember that I forgot to pull the shade down this time. That woman is watching. She is wearing the mink coat even though it is a hot day. She smiles at me but it is not a friendly smile.

I begin to cry. I crawl on my hands and knees to the door. Stella opens it. What are you doing, Martha?

Nothing. I don't feel good. I look up at her.

You're feverish, says Stella, bending down and putting her lips to my forehead. Stella, who is wearing an apron printed with tulips, smells cool and sweet, like a garden.

I knew that I had to continue
firing with the rest regardless
of bodily discomfort.
Pte. M.G.

One of those awful Sundays. Hot, and I have chicken pox. I wake into the long afternoon, feverish, itchy. But I can't scratch, because if I do I'll have pock marks all over my face like Stella's brother, whose family didn't know enough to put cotton mittens on his hands. I want to ask Agnes to take the mittens off. I'll promise not to scratch.

I remember that Agnes is taking Essy and Donald to a birthday party. I must be all alone in the house. It's so quiet I can hear my own heart beating. It's all mixed up with the sound of the cicadas that seems to grow and diminish and grow again inside my head. A hot summer sound, a fever sound. Someone laughs. It that my father? Is he here? When I stand up, I'm dizzy.

I go into the hall. Whispers are coming from the den. Behind the closed door, something is rustling. It is as if the papers have escaped from that drawer and are fluttering all over the room, like birds. What if they get out? I run to the door, I lean on it, I cry, Don't! Don't!

There are more rustling sounds. I move backward across the hall, staring at the door. It opens and Stella comes out. Her hair is hanging loose, the top of her dress is buttoned wrong. She closes the door behind her and leans against it. Then she moves toward me. I'm sitting down now, crying into my cotton mittens. Stella kneels next to me, puts her arms around me.

There, there, she says. Shhhh.

I whisper, My father, my father...

Come, says Stella, and leads me back to my room. She sits beside me, whispering over and over, Your father is fine, he is fine, until I fall asleep.

I wake, frightened still. Agnes is sitting next to my bed.

Stella says, The fever broke.

I say, There was whispering...

She was delirious, says Stella.

I thought something was happening to my father, I sob.

Mouths of babes, says Agnes, but she is not looking at me. She is looking at Stella, who turns away. A rude thing to do when you are spoken to, I think, as I move into sleep again.

For five hours the shelling continued.
Pte. M. G.

If this were a fairy tale, I tell myself, I would be the one to undo the evil spell, even though I am the oldest. Donald seems to be good, but sometimes his green eyes minnow away from mine as if in shame.

Essy would never qualify for spell-undoer. She has a horrible temper and it is getting worse. She throws things, vases and hairbrushes and books, anything. She spills glasses of milk on purpose, she throws mashed potatoes at Stella, she breaks mirrors, she even put her foot through the back screen door one day and said damn. If she were in a fairy story and a dwarf came up to her in the forest and asked her to share her food with him, she would probably kick him. She would never kiss the frog that would turn into a prince. I would. Then everything would be wonderful. For instance, the crayfish I brought back from the cottage last summer would never have died on the back porch in a cake of ice because I forgot them.

One day, I have a curious experience. I am sitting on the davenport when I feel it detach itself from the wall and float free of the rest of the house, of the oatmeal colored wallpaper, the rug, the floor, and me. It is silly, I tell myself, to be surprised that it is a separate thing, because I already knew that, really.

I feel lonely.

A barrage of such intensity
that the very trenches rocked
like a ship in a storm.
      Pte. M. G.

Agnes and my father and Essy and I went on a picnic. Donald stayed home with Stella because he was sick. Father hauled the back seat out of the car and put it on the grass for Essy and me to sit on.

Smile, Martha, smile, Essy, he said, and he took pictures of us sitting there with our cheeks full of deviled egg.

Smile, Mommy, he said, but she wouldn't. She kept her lips tight together and pretended she had to keep the wind from blowing the red-checked tablecloth away.

After lunch, Agnes fell asleep curled in a tree root with Essy next to her, both stomach up, the tips of their fingers just touching. The sky was blue. The fields were full of chicory and Queen Anne's lace.

My father and I went for a walk, holding hands. At the edge of a cliff, we looked over. Far beneath us, water moved over and around flat green rocks. The cold breath of the water surprised me. I stepped back. My father laughed and said he was going to jump over the edge.   He was still laughing as he slid over. He was hanging onto a tree root as thick as my wrist and he made me beg him, Daddy, don't, please, please. A wind came, carrying the red cloth like a sail, straight for him. His face turned white. For a moment, the cloth fluttered between us. When it went, he was on his knees in the grass. He jumped to his feet and bowed. He put a finger to his lips and then to mine.   Old Standby, he whispered. I picked up the cloth and we went back to Essy and Agnes.

Why are you crying, Martha? said Essy.

She *is* crying, said Agnes, looking at my father.

He said, She had a little fall. She's alright now. Right, honey?

I nodded.

The relief could not get through
and we would have to stand off
an attack.
     Pte. M. G.

Father hated to visit Grandmother Brandt. Usually, Agnes and Essy and I and sometimes Donald, would go without him. Grandmother's living room was dark because of the tall trees that grew close to the house. It had never occurred to her, Agnes said, to have a tree or so removed or cut back. The woman just let life grow up around her and didn't raise a finger to control it.

Grandmother always asked me to sit down at the piano and play hymns for her. The one she liked best went like this—I walked in the garden alone, while the dew was still on the roses...I liked the chorus—And he walks with me and he talks with me and he tells me I am his own...On and on it went and when it was over, Grandmother would ask me to please sing it again. I pretended that it was boring, to please Agnes, who couldn't even stay in the room while this went on, but busied herself straightening out the mess in the kitchen or the bedrooms. The truth was, I loved to sing that hymn. I imagined myself walking with my father next to the iris bed in the garden at home, except that I was not myself, but the chrome lady with her chrome hair lifting in a wind. She sat on top of our radio in the dining room. My father had given it to Agnes for a birthday, but Agnes said she didn't like it.

I was shaking as with a chill
  Pte. M. G.

Gladys and I are sitting in her garden in the rose trellis with the facing seats. Gladys is telling the story of how her mother got chosen as the most beautiful girl on the streetcar while she was going to work long ago when she was a secretary for Gladys' father. She is telling it to the jingle jangle of the player piano. I like sitting here, listening to Gladys, who adds something new to her stories each time she tells them. I like hearing Two Little Girls In Blue from the open windows of the big house. Marnie, the maid, is pumping away at the player piano because Gladys' mother is downtown shopping. Marnie does this every chance she gets, shrieking out the words in her big crazy voice. It is as if the music makes her think she's the one who owns the house and the rugs and the maroon velvet drapes that Gladys' mother flings open every morning as if the living room is a stage. When I stay overnight, I try to be downstairs to see this. Gladys' mother is very beautiful, and she is dramatic, that's what Agnes says.

There's a shiny blue glass ball in the middle of the garden on a cement pedestal. I imagine it's an eye. I see myself and Gladys reflected there, two tiny figures. At the back of the garden, next to the big tent where Giles the gardener lives all summer, Gladys' father had a miniature golf course built, with a plywood castle and lots of little bridges. It's a creepy place because of the funeral grass that covers the ground and leaves big spaces where the cracks in the earth show through. I had lost my grandmother's gold heart pin down one of those cracks and I hadn't dared tell Agnes. Gladys' father has two tennis courts behind the golf course. Two tennis courts are vulgar, almost as bad as the golf course. That's what Agnes says and she got it from Gladys' grandmother, Mrs. Dee, who is respected by everyone because of having attended a boarding school run by a French woman.

Mrs. Dee wears French heels, very high and thin, which make her trip on the flagstones in her garden. She uses French perfume and sometimes says things in French. Agnes says Mrs. Dee's French sounds Irish to her. Still, even Agnes is impressed by her. No one except her daughter and granddaughter calls her anything but Mrs. Dee, even Agnes, her very best friend and confidant. Fine reddish hairs stand up like little electric wires all along the sinewy arms of Mrs. Dee. She speaks in a loud, high voice, no matter where she is, as if she would like everyone to understand that however fortunate she may appear, she has nothing to hide from anyone, ever. She loathes Gladys' father, she can't understand how her daughter could have married a vulgar German who has his initials painted in gold on the door of his gray Auburn. She says that he and Giles drive off in that car every single night, into the city to carouse at some low speakeasy. Giles sits in front at first, she says, with his chauffeur's cap on, and then, just outside of town, Giles stops the car and

Gladys' father steps out and gets in front with Giles, who tosses his cap into the back seat. They both light cigars, says Mrs. Dee, and off they go, two bravos laughing like a pair of hyenas.

Two buddies off on a toot, says Mrs. Dee, biting down hard on toot, two buddies off on a toot, drinking whiskey out of chipped cups in some cheap dive, and who knows what else they're up to. Whatever it is, there are floozies involved and it's against the law, she says in a voice that sounds like someone else's, someone who never had been near Mlle Dupont's School for Young Ladies.

In Mrs. Dee's library, a white marble bust of Psyche is supported by a black marble pedestal. I narrow my eyes to try to see the rest of Psyche in the pedestal. Gladys says she's in there, sweating to get out. Gladys says it must be awful to have to stare all day at those gold titles on the backs of the leather books in the shelves, especially if you want to get out to the garden to do nasty things with the garden gnomes. They're all along Mrs. Dee's garden path, painted in bright colors.

Gladys is a different person at her grandmother's. She is quiet, respectful, and she tries to be neat. The only trouble is that her hair stays messy, greasy and wild. It never looks right, and Mrs. Dee says that she got it from her father's side of the family. Gladys' grandmother washes Gladys' hair every time she visits, and sets it in rag curlers, but it still won't look right. Stubborn, Mrs. Dee calls it.

Psyche has blank white eyes. Maybe she's blind. I walk round and round her while Mrs. Dee and Agnes talk in whispers in the parlor. The story about Gladys' father murdering his first wife may have started right here in this house. I have no doubt at all that he did it, says Mrs. Dee.

It's impossible for her to maintain a whisper. She tries, but her voice strives toward its natural level, growing louder with every word. Why in heaven's name, she shouts, would a young woman like that die of a heart attack? It would have been easy for him to do it—he manufactures that funeral grass and those cheap ribbons. He has access to all sorts of chemicals. It would be simple for him, if he tired of a wife, to slip a little something into the bathtub gin.

Agnes, too late, gets up and closes the door between the parlor and the library.

A line of the advancing mass
would fall, others waver for
an instant, then come on with
redoubled fury.
                    Pte. M.G.

Maybe it's the smell of chemicals that's so exciting at Gladys'. The two of us play with those cheap wide colorful ribbons on the back porch, while the blue globe watches. The stiff ribbons can be used for wrapping gift packages, but they are really for decorating funeral wreaths. Gladys wears them in her hair, except when she visits her grandmother. The ribbons smell funny. That must be chemicals. The golf course smells that way too and it's hot back there and those crazy plywood buildings make it look like a cartoon graveyard.

The lily pond, built by Giles of big stones set in concrete, smells of chemicals too. Gladys and I swim among the lily pads. From the pond, wet hair streaming over my eyes, I stare at the garden trees. They look like the Greek ruins in a book in Mrs. Dee's library. On the surface of the pond, the water breaks into oriental script, also in Mrs. Dee's library.

It is impossible to stay away from Gladys'. Everything in the garden and in that house fascinates me. I stare at the shiny side of a tin lunch pail on which rabbits in suits and dresses are busy with Easter eggs. This pail sits on top of the icebox in the back pantry off the porch of Gladys' house. It is exactly like one I have at home, but here it is as marvelous as a Fabergé egg, which I have also seen in one of Mrs. Dee's books.

Marnie's at the piano again. In A Little Spanish Town, this time. I'm afraid of Marnie. I hate to see her crazy wild flushed face at the window, looking out at the garden.

Giles' tent is circus size. Through the flap I can see bright colors and something shiny, but I won't go in. Gladys says Giles came from a circus, he was a tattoo artist, a spieler, a con man. Sometimes she says he's half man, half woman, and a sword swallower. Gladys says he has tattoos, she won't say where. Come in and see, she whispers. If you let him touch you...She laughs her wild laugh that turns me hot and cold with knowing that Gladys sees right through me, every thought and feeling.

*....Frightful stumbling and groping
over shell holes and dead bodies.
      Pte. M.G.*

I feel like a spy paid by Mrs. Dee and Agnes in chocolate cake and peanut butter sandwiches. Also, I can look at Mrs. Dee's books whenever I like. Some of the heavy pages are uncut. Mrs. Dee gives me a letter opener and shows me how to slit them very carefully.

I'm allowed to wander wherever I want to in Mrs. Dee's garden, listening to the two women who sit talking at the wrought iron garden table. Not that I've ever told them anything.

Agnes says, I think Gladys makes up stories, Martha. What in later years I recognize as euphemism is thick as what we call Canadian flies and what the Canadians over the border call American flies. They sift through the screens like ectoplasm, says my father, and they draw blood.

You'd better take anything Gladys says with a grain of salt, Agnes tells me one day. She exaggerates, doesn't she?

When I say, Mmmmm, I can feel how Agnes would like to shake me, lay me out flat on the floor, like the Sunday funnies spread on the German oriental. Even the air of the house fills with the funny paper's tiny dots, the color of everything shifting out of its margins just a little if you look up quick. The radio is on to the

Symphony of the Air. Uncle Flavius, in his shirtsleeves, is standing in the middle of the room, eyes closed, directing the music. His wife is asleep in the blue chair, sitting straight up. Agnes goes into the kitchen, closes the door. The house is too small for the smell of the Sunday pork roast. Probably Agnes breaks that dish out there on purpose.

Some men were crying softly,
not with fear, but with gladness
    Pte. M. G.

That summer, Mrs. Dee and Agnes spend a lot of time sitting in the rose trellis in Mrs. Dee's garden, talking about Gladys' father, until it is so dark the garden gnomes have all disappeared. The two women look like witches there in the fading light, steam rising from their teacups. The whole town is talking by now about how he murdered his first wife.

Gladys never mentions it. In the other trellis, in Gladys' garden, she whispers to me— Sister Anne, Sister Anne, can you see anyone coming?

A puff of smoke, I say, a cloud of dust.

We're staring into the blue garden globe. Gladys' father is in there, tiny, coming our way, smoking a cigarette. Gladys adores him. She calls him the Big Shot. It's what he calls himself. She also calls him Blue Balls. She got that from Giles and it's a secret.

At this time of year, the end of summer, the garden seems to be breaking into flakes, drifting away. The cabbage butterflies spring straight out of the ground. If I lie on my back in the grass, the gold leaves high up in the trees look as if they are peeling off the cloudless blue sky, like bits of the old religious paintings my father took me to see at the art gallery. He held my hand while we stood on the cold marble floor and my toes shriveled in my sneakers.

By the end of that summer, I knew a lot. Something about the way Mrs. Dee and Agnes look at me makes me feel they would like to split me open like one of the sweet-smelling peaches from Mrs. Dee's dwarf tree, to get at what I won't tell them. The women slice the fruit on the garden table with pearl-handled knives from France. The thin hands of the women are freckled and jumpy. My hands look fat next to them, like the children's in Hansel and Gretel.

Soon gentle hands were placing
me on a stretcher.
        Pte. M. G.

When I stay overnight at Gladys', we creep into her parents' big bedroom at the back of the house when they are away. From the window we can look into the dark garden. It is possible to see, in the blue globe, a reflection of whatever is happening in Marnie's room behind the kitchen. That is what we tell each other at any rate, though anything I've seen there is so small from that distance that it is impossible to be sure. It is Gladys who claims she can see exactly what goes on. She says that because I wear glasses, I miss a lot.

Because I can't tell what I'm supposed to see, I rapidly lose interest in the game of watching. I'd rather lie on Gladys' mother's bed and eat chocolates from the drawer of the bedside table. They are delicious chocolates in little stiff crinkled gold cups and it is lovely to lie there and let the sweet taste spread in your mouth and look at the shape of the yellow satin chaise longue against the night sky that's almost white. The grass must be white in the moonlight too. The chaise looks like a woman's body against the sky. If I half close my eyes, I can make it seem to breathe. I imagine the blue glass globe, watching. I sleepily picture the exercycle in the attic and I half dream it hovering over the garden like the big gas balloon my father sent up on the fourth of July.

Sister Anne, sister Anne, I whisper, what do you see?

Just Marnie, says Gladys, she's staring out the window, she's naked. She's listening.

How can you tell, from there?

I just can.

I close my eyes and imagine it. Marnie's smile that slips to one side, her eyes that look right through you, even more than Gladys' do. All the maids in town are farmers' daughters. Everyone says that their fathers are richer than anyone. The minute those girls are old enough, their fathers send them off to other men's houses to earn their keep. They all get five dollars a week, Thursday evenings off and room and board, and they give their fathers most of the five dollars. Marnie is different. Marnie is part Indian. That's what Gladys says. Gladys loves her. She and Giles and Gladys play three-handed solitaire at night in the breakfast nook under the overhead bulbs shaped like flames.

Long after dark, you can hear the tonk-a-tonk of tennis balls from the courts. When it stops, it means they're coming back, and that's when we go back to Gladys' room.

When did it stop? I sit up. Come on, I say, we better go.

Wait. Hear that?

The back door opening.

Oh boy, someone's leaving. Marnie's back at the window, Gladys reports. There was someone in there with her all the time she was naked! Oh, oh, guess what? It's your father!

My stomach turns over.   It's not! It's *your* father! Everyone knows about that!

Uh uh, it's yours—old lover-boy, come and see— he's tucking his shirt in, he's coughing.

I hear the cough. Is it my father's? I can't tell. Gladys is trying to pull me over to the window. Look! Look!

I keep my eyes closed.   You're lying. You're a liar!

You were afraid to look! Gladys holds her sides and rocks back and forth, laughing in a spluttering sort of way.   Now she's rolling on the floor, still laughing, shouting it now, shrieking as if she's gone crazy.

You made it up! You made it up! I yell.

I can hear the grownups out there in the dark now, coming up the path from the tennis court. I can hear my mother laugh. Gladys, still on her back on the floor, sticks her tongue out. I kick her, hard.

His eyes had that glassy
look that means death.
Pte. M. G.

Chloroform! How did she get chloroform? Agnes shouts.

From the medicine cupboard. She chased me with it. She said she was going to kill me.

Oh my god, chloroform! Come with me! I want her grandmother to hear this!

She's a liar, I sob. She says you can see everything in that blue ball!

Chloroform! says Mrs. Dee, Mon Dieu! That man has chloroform in the house! The two women exchange glances. So do the garden gnomes. Psyche strains to free her self.

I don't want to talk. I'm trembling. They give me peanut butter cookies and fudge.

Did you ever see the things Gladys talks about?

Just once. His, his arm, reaching up to turn off the light.

Whose arm?

His—her father's.

What light was it?

The one over Marnie's bed.   I'm lying, but I don't care.

Mon Dieu! Mon Dieu!

Next day I have measles. While I'm sick, Gladys is sent away to boarding school. I think about the fun we used to have playing with those ribbons on the back porch. When Gladys' mother dies of a heart attack, Gladys is still away at school. She comes home briefly. I see her across the room at the funeral, holding Mrs. Dee's hand and smiling. She looks blurred. It is as if I'm seeing her through rain, in a window, like Marnie.

A shadow seemed to pass over
the tired face...and another
soul had "gone west."
    Pte. M. G.

Agnes is not a shouting person, but she is shouting
now, at my father. Do you want to be a good boy all your
life, for god's sake? she yells. I listen from my room,
where I am drawing pictures. Agnes shouts, They are
killing you! And you're letting them do it! The den door
slams and I can't hear what my father says.

Later, when they have both gone out, I creep into
the den. The wastebasket is filled with the articles my
father wrote for PEPANDGO. I take the shiny papers
out of the basket and smooth them. I wonder why Agnes
threw them away. My father would never do such a thing.
He is proud of those articles. My favorite of them all has
been torn into tiny, tiny bits and it takes a long time to get
them together so that I can read what it says. I don't even
know if my father wrote this one—it doesn't have his
name on it. It says, "We regret to announce the death of a
loyal, faithful agent, Mr. Norbert Allen. Mr. Allen was
known to the sporting world as the One-Legged Bicycle
Rider. He came with us in 1915 and has been a steady,
consistent producer. He has done more to bring the need
of insurance to his friends and circus folks than any other
agent." It's hard to read the words now, but I know them
by heart anyway. I put everything back in the waste-paper

basket when I finish. Then I do what I tell myself later was a crazy thing. I'm on my hands and knees on the floor and I bend over and kiss the overflowing basket. I feel myself growing hot with embarrassment and I take a quick look out the window, but no one is watching.

That night, I dream about the one-legged bicycle rider, but it is horrible. He is coming apart. His other leg falls off, and then his arms, and he is still riding the bicycle. When he turns his face to look at me, his nose is gone. I wake up screaming. I'm not entirely well yet. That's what Stella says.

I am sitting on my bedroom floor on a Numdah rug, drawing. I cover a sheet of paper with black crayon. As if by magic, from the right margin, a face begins to emerge. It is a woman. I am astounded. I stare back at the face. I did not put it there, and yet, there it is. I black it out, but I cannot forget it.

A whistle sounded, a bell rang,
and the long train started on
its trip to the coast.
        Pte. M. G.

It was a day like any other, a fact that frightened me for a long time afterward. I came home from school. When I opened the side door I knew that something had happened. It was the awful thing I had been expecting, though I hadn't realized until this moment that I had been waiting for it for a long time now.

No one home, and yet the door is unlocked. Inside, a smell of strangers. The rugs rumpled. The oatmeal wallpaper on the stairway wall torn, as if something hard had bumped against it.

I walk straight up the stairs, past the desk and the bowl of teeth and stones and the feather pen, right into my parents' room. The door is open, the rugs disordered. The mattress on Agnes's bed is crooked. The drawer of the table between the beds is open and the gun is gone.

I think, well, it is over. Not it's over, but IT IS OVER, with each word, which has waited so long to be said, given its due.

Pretty soon I am sitting in my father's armchair next to the bookcase in the living room, holding the gray cat in my lap. Stella comes in. Her face is red, her eyes are puffy, her hair is falling over her face. She looks terrible, fat and old. She is not pretty at all now.

Stella tries to smile. She says, You're going to have dinner at the Reynolds'. Essy and Donald are there already. Come— she says, and holds out her hand. But I draw back into the chair. I shake my head. I turn to stone. I am very strong, and so heavy that no one can move me from this chair or this house. The cat will scratch Stella if she comes too close.

The sound of a car in the driveway. Stella wipes her hands on her apron and goes out to the kitchen. I listen to the side door opening. NOW, I tell myself. It is as if I am waiting for a play to begin.

Agnes comes in. She is crying, her head on Charlotte's shoulder. Charlotte is guiding her steps, as if Agnes is blind. I have never seen my mother behave this way before. I think,   My father is dead.

His supply of typing paper is next to me in the bookshelf. As long as I can remember, I have been forbidden to touch this paper. I ask Charlotte, in a loud voice, if I may use my father's paper.

Charlotte looks at me. Agnes does not seem to know I am here. Charlotte says,   Yes, it's all right, now.

I am alone again. I remove some paper from the shelf. I pick up my father's fountain pen, which is next to the paper. The cat is on the floor now, blinking up at me. I draw a cat, a simple one, the kind I used to draw when I was very young.

I close my eyes and sit quietly. Ah, I whisper, ah. Ah, I say, louder now.

I am quiet again. I do not move. I have never noticed before that this house has always been filled with sound. Now there is none from the kitchen, where Stella must be. The Westminster chimes clock on the fireplace mantel is not ticking. Agnes must have forgotten to wind it this morning. There is no sound from upstairs. The cat is nowhere to be seen.

I stare at the dancing dust motes in the sunlight that is pouring in through the windows. The chairs and tables, the player piano, are blurred by its brilliance. The walls have vanished. It is as if the house has become enormous, as big as the whole world. My mouth is dry. Now I can hear the furnace whispering in the cellar. Ahhhhh, it breathes, ahhhhh, shhhhhh, shhhhhh.

I hold my breath. I close my eyes and feel the room grow small again. The crayoned face of the woman flickers on the inside of my eyelids like one of my father's home movies.

I take a breath and open my eyes. I see my own hand on the paper in my lap, the fingers still holding my father's pen. I turn the picture over and make a diagonal slash on the back of the paper with the pen.

I begin to cry. Under the davenport, the cat's tongue rasps over fur and skin.

I dreamed that we were
on the march bound for
the trenches.
        Pte. M. G.

When Agnes had to go to work running the insurance business, she compared herself with her own mother, who had just given up and never raised a hand to do anything except make those olive sandwiches when her husband died. Agnes hated the whole idea of insurance, which she claimed encouraged attitudes which were going to ruin the world, and she never expected to have to do anything like this, but there was no one else to take over and that was that.

There would, she said, be no money if she didn't go to work. This would not have been so if it had not been for my Great Uncle Oscar, the idiot savant. When Agnes' beloved grandfather was very old, he had approached her with a plan to which she was free to agree or not. He would abide by her decision. He told her that he was thinking of leaving his entire fortune to Agnes's cousin, Oscar, who was also his grandchild. Oscar, as a child, would come home and play on the piano the entire concert his parents had taken him to hear, but he would never be able to take care of himself. Agnes's grandfather said that Oscar was not like other people because his mother, who was Agnes' Aunt Jennifer, had whooping cough when she was pregnant with him. This Aunt

Jennifer was the one who fell in love with a very rich and prominent man after she was married and had given birth to her idiot savant son. Everyone, even her husband, who traveled because he worked for the government, and even her mother, the horrible mean grandmother of Agnes' stories, understood this, because of Aunt Jennifer's beauty and her sorrow about her son. When she had a breast removed, the rich man used to spend hours with her, rubbing her arm, which was very painful. Agnes remembered seeing this.

Of course, Agnes agreed to her grandfather's plan. As he pointed out himself, she was well provided for by her husband, whose agency was the most profitable in the country, while poor Oscar, the idiot savant, spent his days in a dark house, playing the piano to a cat.

It was an endless march,
and we seemed to move unconsciously,
as if impelled by some hidden force.
        Pte. M. G.

Aunt Emmy decided to sell insurance for Agnes. She bought herself a little Ford and that's how it was that one day, because the door didn't lock properly on the passenger side, she accidentally dropped her son-in-law's mother out on the Parkway along with a huge amount of toilet paper they'd just bought on sale. His mother wasn't hurt in the least, and Richard never dared say a word. His mother was a shy little farm lady and she was so impressed by Aunt Emmy that she didn't seem to mind at all what had happened. Agnes claimed that the poor woman was flattered to death to become a part of one of Aunt Emmy's anecdotes.

Another result of Aunt Emmy's purchase of the car was that she and Agnes could now carry dolls and letters and the serial stories Coletta and I were writing, back and forth every single day except for Sunday. That first summer, there were parties in the garden under the peach tree for one or the other of Coletta's visiting dolls, just about every week.

Those frightful hordes of Germans
were advancing once more.
Again I was buried and unable to move.
　　Pte. M.G.

Pepita is in the garden, at the back, past the iris bed and the rose trellis that is smaller than the one in Gladys' garden and larger than the one in Mrs. Dee's. Pepita is near the tree that had the tent caterpillars that fell onto my head last year. I stood on the rustic table screaming until Stella came running from the house with my father's old black umbrella. Even that umbrella did not stop my shivering with disgust and terror as I walked back to the house, while Stella kept assuring me that the caterpillars were out of my hair. A lot has happened since then. Mrs. Dee has put her house up for sale in order to move near Gladys' boarding school. Gladys' father has sold his house and given the tennis courts to the neighborhood. No one knows where he is. I am ten now and have learned not to scream.

Pepita is one of my dolls. Her exact location at the moment is under the lilac bush behind the garage near the gooseberry and red currant bushes. I push vines and branches aside and stare at the doll, flat on its back, with a maple leaf from the Robertson's tree next door covering its chest. Pepita's nose has gone soft in the rain. It looks like those caterpillars. If I pressed the nose, it would be spongy. I allow the branches and vines to snap back in place.

I hurry into the house by way of the back stairs, through the pantry, into the kitchen. I hear sounds from Stella's room. I go in without knocking and say, to Stella's back, because she is making her own bed, Oh, poor Pepita, where is she? My voice catches where my tonsils still are.

Stella turns and looks at me. Her lower lip is trembling. Her pale hair is drawn back into a bun. She has beautiful, delicate skin, but she smells of the kitchen—that's what Agnes says.

I stare at the shiny blue edge of the Old Granger tobacco packet that shows from under her pillow. I keep a packet like that with a little tobacco in it in my sock drawer, to remind me of my father.

Did you look everywhere? Stella turns to move the pillow. The packet doesn't show now. She pulls the chenille spread over the pillow.

I say, Yes, and I just know that awful dachshund took her, I just know it! Stupid dog!

Stella says, Now, now.

My hair, like my father's, is dark and has the smooth, composed look of oriental hair. My skin, also like his, is dark, especially in the summer, and I have my father's shiny blue eyes. My face, like his, is pink at the top of the cheekbones. I turn my head in such a way that I know will allow the light from the window to shine on my cheek. From the corner of my eye, I watch a tear slip down Stella's cheek. A thrill turns over and over at the bottom of my stomach.

*—Only to find that I was holding
the Doctor's arm in a powerful grip
and yelling at the top of my voice.
        Pte. M. G.*

On the day I decide to find Pepita, I stand there
staring down at the doll, saying over and over, my god,
my god, oh my god. Jesus, I say, Jesus Christ almighty! I
start on a whisper and get louder, but not loud enough for
anyone to hear. I love the way the words feel. The more
I say them, the more I believe that I am really finding
Pepita for the first time. When I believe it enough, I
shout— Pepita!

Stella comes running to see. So does Essy.

Essy goes on and on about Pepita's hair—It's
gone, it's all gone, oh, where is it? Her eyes dart here,
there. She's scared, she knows very well what must have
happened—the dachshund ate that wig. I'm forgetting
fast that I was the one who left Pepita under the lilac bush
just to see what would happen. I'm so sorry for myself
my ears are ringing.

Everything that dachshund does to us is Essy's
fault and she knows it. It is because of something that
happened to her doll, Margery, a big stupid-looking
creature with a face and hands of composition. The cloth
body, arms and legs of Margery are filled with straw that
you can hear shifting around in a dumb aimless way
whenever Margery is moved. Margery is missing a finger

on her left hand. It was chewed off by that dachshund while Essy just stood there crying with her eyes shut. She should have chased him away. I would have. Essy made that dog think it could do anything it wanted to this family. Ever since that day, bad things have happened to us. I stare at Essy, with this thought huge in my head and in my eyes.

Essy looks frantic. She seems to be dissolving. She may wet her pants, like Donald. She looks like the little Match Girl. Her posture is terrible. Her hair, which is supposed to resemble Shirley Temple's (that's what Agnes says anyway) really looks like cooked spaghetti. Essy looks like Agnes. Some people think that's pretty.

His bandage has slipped,
showing a face battered
and torn beyond description.
        Pte. M. G.

Bald Pepita and I are watching Essy, who is
running past the house behind a wicker doll buggy
containing Margery, who is wearing a maroon velvet coat
with a rabbit fur collar and large round buttons that look
as dumb as Margery. It is the second time Essy has gone
by, crying and screaming. She is being chased by a skinny
orange cat. I am watching from the living room, kneeling
on the davenport and staring through the front window.

Margery has not been invited to the party Pepita is
giving under the peach tree in the garden. Stella's sister's
doll, Looloo, is coming. So is a doll named Vivian Loretta,
who belongs to Coletta. I am giving the party to celebrate
Pepita's return. No one associated with that dachshund is
allowed to come. This party is special. Pepita, thanks to
her stay in the garden, seems to have gained some extra
power. I have heard about Lazarus from a friend who has
a huge collection of colored cards that are given to the
children in the Methodist Sunday School. Pepita gives me
the creeps. I've never trusted her. Her name for instance.
Where did it come from? It seems to just be part of her,
like her painted-on eyes. Those eyes are scary. I don't like
to look at them. It feels as if they know something nasty
about me. Pepita is a cloth doll, but she is stuffed so

tightly that she is nearly as hard as a composition doll. She is stained with mud and water, but now that she has dried out, she's as solid as she was before, still neatly stitched along her arms and legs and up the sides of her body and face. Margery has eyes that open and shut with a click that makes my teeth ache. Pepita's painted-on eyes simply stare in a way that has nothing to do with the paint that flaked off during her suffering in the garden. I chip off more paint while waiting for Essy to reappear out there. I remove almost the whole of one eye, and just as I suspected, the stare remains. If I not only removed both eyes, but burned Pepita in the fireplace, that stare would still exist.

Gradually the shell-swept areas
were replaced by fresh green fields
and peaceful cottages with smoke curling
up from their chimneys. The roar of the
guns died away in the distance.
and all was calm and peaceful.
        Pte. M.G.

Stella is worried about Essy. She says, "Why won't you let Margery come to your party, Martha?

I say, Pepita doesn't want her. I clutch the doll to me and look up at Stella. I look at her in the way I remember my father looking at people. Stella stares back. She makes a little whimpering sound.

I turn away from Stella and remove Pepita's other eye. Stella whispers, Oh, you are cruel.

Stella is dying to stay on here. She doesn't want to go back to that dismal old farmhouse. That's what Agnes said to Mrs. Dee. I'm just waiting for an excuse to let her go, she told Mrs. Dee.

No one could blame you for that, said Mrs. Dee.

To tell the truth, I feel sorry for her.

Don't, said Mrs. Dee.

As if she knows what I am thinking, Stella stands there, doing nothing. Then she shakes her head. I don't care, she says, and runs out to rescue Essy. She squats next to her on the sidewalk, talking. The orange cat sits in the grass, washing itself. When they come in, Stella is carrying the cat. She calls it a stray. She says that she and

Essy are going to give it some milk. Essy and Margery follow Stella to the kitchen.

I wonder what my mother will say about bringing in a dirty old cat like that, I call after them.

All the rest of that morning, while I am getting ready for the party, Stella is teaching Essy to get along with the cat. I pass Essy in the pantry on my way to the garden. She is sitting in a patch of sunlight. Margery is propped against the cupboard with her eyes half closed. One lid goes down further than the other, and this gives her a crazy look. Essy is hugging the cat, which is purring.

Excuse me, I say. My arms are full of Coletta's doll, Vivian Loretta. Agnes had brought the doll from the office last night. Vivian Loretta is a large, spoiled-looking beauty in a pink silk dress. She has a gift for Pepita, a small muff, which I recognize as being cut from the fur of a famous coat of Aunt Emmy's, bought by her on the day she also bought a new dress, shoes and a hat, all of which she put on. She sent the old things to Doctor's office with a note reading, BODY TO FOLLOW. This was when they first came from Nicaragua and Emmy believed life might continue as it had before. The coat was attacked by moths, and that's why it had been cut up, for instance, into a little jacket for Coletta that looks terrible on her. Miranda says it would look good if she would stand up straight, like me.

It's a nice sunny day for the party. The table under the peach tree is set with dishes of Hungarian goulash, which is a mixture of weeds and leaves and berries left in water in fruit jars in the sun. There are also real peanut butter cookies made by Stella, and air tea.

Stella's little sister Tweetie has brought her doll to the party. It is a battered celluloid kewpie decorated with pink feathers and sequins. Probably she won it at the county fair. This doll has brought a gift of a necklace which is made of Christmas tree ornament glass. It is also from the fair, the booby prize for not really winning at the fishing game. Tweetie is not interested in dolls. She pretends she is because she admires me. Tweetie's nose is always running, even now, in summer.

Tweetie is about the same age as Essy, but she knows better than to pay any attention to Essy, who is sitting on the edge of the sandbox across the yard, watching. She is holding Margery in one arm and the orange cat in the other.

I am being very kind to Tweetie, who does not know how to behave at a party. Tweetie makes her doll reach across the table for a cookie. Her doll says, in a high, silly voice, Hey, I don't have no sugar in my tea. Tweetie says, in her own voice—Boy, who spit in the goulash? and she laughs and laughs. I say, just the way Agnes would—It is only a snail, dear. And I remove it.

I have been noticing that the orange cat is hissing. Essy, of course, is holding it much too tightly. She is also trying to eat the cookie Stella gave her. After a while, the cat escapes and comes over to the party table, maybe hoping for some crumbs. Kitty, kitty, kitty, Essy calls, but not as if she expects it to do any good. The cat pays no attention. I pretend to ignore it. The cat moves closer. When I stand to put a balloon back on a branch of the peach tree, the cat begins to wind itself around my legs. I push it away. When I sit down again, it jumps into my lap, curls up, and goes to sleep. Essy sits banging her heels against the side of the sandbox, bang, bang, bang.

After the party, when Tweetie has gone home, Essy tries to coax the cat back. It turns on her and chases her into the house and up onto the back of the davenport. Essy's face turns bright red and she screams and screams until Stella rescues her.

Later that day, I put Pepita into a department store box and take the box to the garden. I begin to dig a hole in the ground near the big red peonies.

What are you doing, Martha?" Essy asks. She is sitting on the back porch steps with Margery.

I go on digging with the spade.   I'm burying Pepita. She's dead, I say.

Essy watches. Margery's big round buttons watch. Essy begins to cry. Now she is making gulping sounds. Oh poor Pepita, she wails, oh poor Pepita, she was lost so long and then she had her party and now she's dead, oh please, she begs, as if I am God, oh please, please!

It annoys me almost unbearably that Essy, like Agnes, always puts into words what is obvious already to everyone. It makes me want to hurt her even more.

Essy sobs and begs, but I will not be moved. I shove the last of the dirt over the box and stamp it down hard. When Stella comes out to comfort her, Essy bites her.

That night, when Agnes comes home from the office, I tell her about the tobacco packet under Stella's pillow. I say, I don't think she ought to have something of my father's in her room. I say, It makes me feel terrible.

The next morning Stella is gone.

After she had left, Agnes discovered Stella's rosary at the back of a drawer. She told me not to touch it. She said she had found one on the street and picked it up on the very day I fell down the stairs when I was two years old and had to have stitches in my head and Agnes was sure I was dead when she found me. She didn't like the way the wallpaper was faded over Stella's bed where that bloody picture of Jesus was hung. I never liked having that girl in the house, she said.

I found myself humming
"The Long Trail"
    Pte. M. G.

    An old lady whose name is Mrs. Bird takes Stella's place. She has trouble climbing stairs. We'll just keep her until we can find someone else, says Agnes.

    I can do anything I want now, all day. I can take Essy and Donald into the den and read what our father wrote about the war to them. Donald doesn't say anything. He doesn't even wet his pants anymore. Essy cries at the scary parts and begs to leave, but I won't let her. I tell them we need to know what happened to our father. I think it's sort of true, but I don't know why.

They cheered as we started up
the Waterloo Road. And all along
the way to the hospital, people
would stop and wave as we went past.
     Pte. M.G.

In Aunt Emmy's bathroom, a bottle of Hinds Honey and Almond Cream is attached to the wall. It is wonderful to me that the cream can be dispensed from that bottle, as if there is an endless supply of the sweet-smelling, miraculously thick and shiny stuff somewhere inside the wall. I always manage to visit the bathroom when I am there and use that dispenser. I walk out sniffing at my delicious hands.

It is weeks now since my father's death. I wander into Aunt Emmy's bedroom. Aunt Emmy is getting dinner in the kitchen and talking to herself. I sit on her bed. I open the big scrapbook she keeps of family photographs, newspaper clippings about the British royal family and a studio portrait of a very good-looking man, a relative, she says, who once was in a movie. It is signed in writing so fancy and now so faded that I have never been able to read it.

I turn the familiar pages and find something I have not seen before. It is a newspaper article about my father's death. It says that he was despondent. It says that he was a prominent businessman. It says that he was injured in the Great War. It says that he used a revolver to shoot himself in his car, out in the countryside.

Aunt Emmy's voice rises from the kitchen. Never mind, darling, she calls, as she always does, never mind. You'll end in Hollywood.

It is as if she is singing.

In the dark room, a flicker of old Christmas, black and white. Stella comes in and comes in with the cake. Camera registers at some length the tiny doppelganger of her, slipping along the shiny hip of a pitcher.

The dark eye of the fireplace watches Martha kneel, bend, lift the box top, smile for the camera, hold up the sweater in front of Donald, who sobs with his mouth open wide. Martha balances the ribbon's bow on his head, grins at the camera. Donald goes on crying.

Uncle Flavius doesn't speak and doesn't speak again to polka-dotted Sophie, shapely as the pitcher. She keeps her knees together tight, tries for primness on a mouth that won't have it, won't.

Bow falls off Donald's head. Father not here, he's the camera, not here, and soon won't be at all. A blur of lit tree against the glass French doors locked on the sun porch, wickered for the summer he won't know.

Snow licks clean the reverberant windows, jitter of window, jitter of Essy, film's gone crazy. At the edges of Sophie, the screen turns white, pulses her Flavius-wary breathing, and begins to burn. Vaguely smiling Charlotte is too polite to notice, even as she herself burns. Cat and Martha fade to Cheshire grins.

Agnes, paling, speeded-up, fire-pursued, touches Salmon's undulant shoulder, quick, quick, smiles at

Sophie, quick, offers tea. Sophie takes it in slow motion, drops it, drops it. Her legs spread. Uncle Flavius falls on her, they burn together. Film dies.

I FELL ASLEEP AND MY DREAM CONTINUED THE PICTURE. IT IS EVENING AND THE SHADOWS ARE SLOWLY STEALING ACROSS THE LAND. GRADUALLY THE TWILIGHT DEEPENS, AND OVER ALL CREEPS A HUSH, BROKEN ONLY BY THE CHIRP OF THE CRICKET OR THE LONELY NOTE OF THE WHIP-POOR-WILL AS HE FLITS OVER THE MEADOW. FAR DOWN THE FIELDS A MIST IS HANGING OVER THE CREEK AND I FANCY I HEAR ITS BABBLING NOISE AS IT TUMBLES OVER THE ROCKS AND PEBBLES. FOR ME, THE "LONG TRAIL" IS ENDED, AND I HAVE REACHED BLIGHTY.

Pte. Martin Gresham

Norma Kassirer lives in Buffalo, New York. *The Hidden Wife*, a collection of her stories with artwork by Willyum Rowe, was published by Shuffaloff Press in 1991. Other stories and poems have appeared in various journals, including Blatant Artifice, Sow's Ear, Yellow Edenwald Field, and elsewhere. Her short story cycle *Milly* was published in 2008 by the Buffalo Ochre Papers.

She has also written two novels for children, both published by the Viking Press: *Magic Elizabeth*, in 1966 (reprinted by Harper and by Knopf and Scholastic, and most recently appearing through Breakfast Serials), and *The Doll Snatchers*, Viking, 1969.

Both of her daughters have long been engaged with writing and publishing, the cover images having been drawn by her daughter Karen as a child.

6658546R0

Made in the USA
Charleston, SC
19 November 2010